I0797191

The
Office
Second Edition

MJF
PUBLISHING

Second Edition

Mike Faricy

This is a work of fiction. All of the characters, organizations, and events portrayed in this novel are either products of the author's imagination or are used fictitiously.

Library of Congress Control Number: 2023915005
paperback ISBN: 978-1-962080-23-1
e-book ISBN: 978-1-962080-24-8

MJF Publishing books may be purchased for education, Business, or promotional use. For information on bulk purchases, please contact the author directly at mikefaricyauthor@gmail.com

Published by

MJF Publishing
https://www.mikefaricybooks.com

To Teresa

“I don’t believe it!”

Acknowledgments

I would like to thank the following people for their help and support:

Special thanks to my editors, Kitty, Donna and Rhonda for their hard work, cheerful patience and positive feedback.

I would like to thank Ann and Julie for their creative talent and not slitting their wrists or jumping off the high bridge when dealing with my Neanderthal computer capabilities.

Special thanks to Ann for her patience.

Last, I would like to thank family and friends for their encouragement and unqualified support. Special thanks to Maggie, Jed, Schatz, Pat, Av, Emily and Pat for not rolling their eyes, at least when I was there, and most of all, to my wife Teresa whose belief, support and inspiration has from day one, never waned.

Prologue

I'd stopped in for just one at The Spot with my attorney and officemate, Louie Laufen. That was two hours ago.

"God, I can't believe it," Louie said. He was off his stool, patting down his trouser pockets and his wrinkled pinstriped suit coat. "I thought for sure I put my wallet in my pocket before we came over."

Mike, the bartender, shot me a look. We were both just as sure he purposely left it in his desk drawer. It seemed to be almost second nature.

"I suppose I could run over and grab it if I can find it," Louie said, giving me a look as he spoke.

"Relax, I'll get it. Go on. You better get out of here if you're going to make that meeting. You can catch me next time."

"You sure, man?"

Like I had an option. "Yeah, I'll get it, no sweat. Hey, Mike," I called. "As long as I'm buying, maybe just one more beer, then cut me off so I get home in one piece."

“See you tomorrow, dude, and thanks,” Louie said. “Hey, I’ve got a court appearance first thing, so I won’t be in until ten, maybe eleven if things go my way.”

“Safe drive home,” I said, grabbing the fresh beer Mike slid across the bar.

As Louie walked out the door, an attractive looking woman stepped in. She was dressed in white shorts that looked like they had been spray-painted on and a halter top that looked a size or two, too small. Her dark hair was pulled back in a ponytail.

“Dev Haskell?” she said, looking at Mike and me. We were the only two people in the bar. It was league play night for The Spot softball team, and the regulars wouldn’t be here until sometime close to 9:00.

“Yeah, that’s me,” I said and took a sip. It looked like my luck was beginning to change.

“Hi, Mr. Haskell. A friend said I should find you, but well, it’s kind of a personal matter. Could I maybe talk to you outside?”

“Mike won’t listen in, and even if he did, he wouldn’t remember,” I said.

“It’s, ahh, of a *very* personal nature. You might find it enjoyable,” she said and sort of looked embarrassed as she fiddled with her thumbs and index fingers.

I was off the stool in a second and standing next to her at the door. She had bright blue eyes that seemed to sparkle, pearly white teeth and a gorgeous complexion. The rest of her wasn’t all that bad either.

She looked me up and down then said, “Mmm-hmm, my friend wasn’t lying. Come on outside, honey, and let’s talk.”

I quickly followed her outside. She walked over to a black Mercedes, an AMG G-63. The windows were tinted so dark I couldn’t see inside. “Here this will give us some privacy,” she said.

My immediate thought was things were really going my way until the rear window was suddenly lowered, and Tubby Gustafson stuck his red nose, the size of a baked potato, out the window. As he did so, the driver’s door swung open, and Fat Freddy Zimmerman hurried around the front of the car, waving a twenty-dollar bill.

“Here you go, Cindy, thanks,” he said and handed the twenty to the woman.

She shoved the bill into her halter top and said, “Not a problem, happy to help.” She didn’t take the time to give me as much as a second look and just walked away.

“Get in,” Tubby said to me, then raised his window.

As Fat Freddy led me around to the driver’s side, I said, “Hey, what’s this about?”

“Come on, man. You should know better than to ask that, just get in,” he said and opened the rear door.

I climbed into the backseat next to Tubby. Fat Freddy slid behind the wheel and put the car in gear.

“Hey, wait, guys, not so fast. I got a tab going in there and a fresh beer on the bar.”

“Amazing. Not.” Tubby said. “And by the way, you’re already trying my patience here. Now, buckle up, Haskell, and please, don’t touch anything.”

“But . . .” The look from Tubby pretty much put a stop to any questions I may have felt like asking.

One

Fat Freddy pulled into a secluded scenic parking area overlooking the Mississippi River. The parking area was surrounded by a three-foot-high limestone wall and then a thick hedge, maybe another two feet higher directly behind the limestone wall. I knew from experience years back that the place was popular after dark with the high school crowd. Freddy parked at the far end, jumped out, and ran around the car to open Tubby's door.

"Pleasure me with your attention, Haskell," Tubby said, and slowly oozed out of the backseat.

I figured that meant I should join him, and I opened the door then walked around to the rear of the car. At the moment, we were the only vehicle in the parking area. A black SUV, I think a Cadillac Escalade, pulled across the entrance, effectively blocking anyone's attempt to enter. Not that anyone was going to try to drive in with the two muscle-bound thugs sitting in the front seat.

"Let's enjoy the view, Haskell," Tubby said and walked toward the bluff. A solid rock wall dropped straight down for maybe thirty feet with a handful of large boulders scattered around the bottom. As a sixteen-year-old, I'd had an unfortunate encounter with root beer flavored schnapps one night in this very spot. I'd never quite recovered, avoiding any and all contact with the stuff for two decades.

"Lovely view, isn't it?" Tubby said. From this distance, the river appeared to flow gently around the bend and then on through the downtown area. "Come over here, Haskell, don't tell me you're afraid of heights."

"No, sir, not at all. I just don't like to tempt fate."

Tubby nodded like this made sense. "Here's the thing, Haskell. Against my better judgment, I'm going to send some business your way. No, no, no. No need to thank me. It's the least I can do. In the past, you've never seemed to fail to disappoint, but foolish me, I'm going to give you yet another opportunity."

"What kind of business are we talking here?"

"A distant acquaintance of mine, a gentleman by the name of Ozzie Frick, will be contacting you tomorrow. Let me thank you in advance for helping him."

"What does he want?"

"That's one of the many reasons you remain so unsuccessful, Haskell. You ask too many questions. You just take care of him, and things will work out."

"But I don't even know what—"

"Haskell, take a look at this," Tubby said and stepped right up next to the edge of the cliff. There was a small rock close to the edge, Tubby kicked it up into the air, and we both focused on it as it sailed off the cliff, then arched downward and bounced off one of the boulders below. "It's such a long way down, and then there's all those boulders, not at all what I'd call comforting. Now, any questions? Good," he answered for me. "Maybe stay here and study the view until it begins to resonate somewhere in that thick skull of yours. I'll expect a full report once you meet with Ozzie. Thank you," he said, then proceeded to walk back to his car.

"Hey, Tub . . . err, ahh, Mr. Gustafson," I called. "Would it be all right if you maybe gave me a lift back to The Spot. See, I've got an important meeting later tonight out in Burnsville, and well, my car is still parked down at The Spot."

Fat Freddy opened the rear door, and Tubby climbed in. Once he had settled into the backseat, Freddy closed the door then smiled, and gave me a little wave.

"Freddy, you can't leave me here. It's like five miles back."

Freddy ignored me, hurried around to the driver's side, and climbed in. I heard the locks on the doors click a moment later, and they drove off with the Escalade following closely behind.

I stepped over to the edge of the cliff. Tubby had been right, it was a long way down. I had five miles to cover before I got back to The Spot, so I started walking.

Two

I woke up early the next morning. Sophie was still asleep. She lay on her side, facing me with her pillow pulled over her head, and the sheet tucked under her arm. I stared for a long moment examining the curve of her hip beneath the sheet, weighing the odds of trying to wake her. I decided it probably wasn't worth the risk. She could have a short fuse from time to time, and past experience had taught me that waking her in the early morning was never going to go my way. I quietly slipped out of bed, stepped into my boxers, and headed out to her living room. Her dog, Lilly, a chocolate lab, sort of half-opened one eye, then wiggled down a little further in her bed and went back to sleep.

Sophie lived in the suburb of Burnsville, on Alimagnet lake, about twenty miles outside of Saint Paul. It was a gorgeous area and a lovely lake. The opposite shore was all parkland and, at this hour of the day, completely quiet. I stared out at the lake through the living room window for a few moments. There was a light fog on the water with the sun just beginning to come over the treetops on the eastern shore. I put the coffee on, then tried to figure out which one of the three remotes turned on the tv. After about ten minutes of pushing different buttons, I gave up, poured myself a mug of coffee, and just sat there, staring out the window.

We'd met a few months back in school, Dog Obedience school. Sophie's dog, Lilly, got first in class, but then Sophie was the instructor. Morton, my Golden retriever, earned a five percent discount ticket should we want to enroll in the beginner's session again. I guess the good news was Sophie and I sort of hit it off. Friends with benefits. We seemed to get together every so often and enjoyed each other's company. We had an unspoken rule that whoever hosted last time was the guest the next time around.

I settled onto the couch and stared out at the lake, sipping coffee, and watching as the fog slowly dissipated. I was obsessing about my upcoming meeting with Tubby's friend Ozzie Frick. I didn't know anything about the man other than Tubby Gustafson basically promised to kill me if I didn't meet with him. Not exactly the best introduction. I figured whatever the guy wanted me to do, I would just tell him it was out of my league. Maybe say something like the Feds were taking an interest in whoever hired me, and it might be in his best interest to get as far away from me as quickly as possible.

I was on my third cup of coffee when I heard the bathroom door close. Sophie wandered into the living room, rubbing the sleep from her eyes a few minutes later. She was dressed in a silk dressing gown, burgundy with white trim. She'd tied her dark hair up in a bun on top of her head, and she was barefoot.

"You okay, Dev? How long have you been up?"

I glanced at the clock sitting on her fireplace mantel. It was just a little after seven.

"I guess a couple of hours. You want me to get you a coffee?"

"No, thanks, baby. I can get it. Anything bugging you? You seemed kind of preoccupied, once you finally got here last night."

"Oh, sorry. I told you about the client I met with last night. I'm not really all that fond of the guy, to begin with, he contacted me and wants me to meet with someone he knows. I don't want—"

"So, tell him no, or tell him you can't because you're too busy."

"Mmm-mmm, no, it's not really that kind of a deal."

"Oh, well, if he's a good customer and he's sending a lot of business your way, maybe you should just do it." She was at the kitchen counter now, filling her coffee mug. I was still staring out at the lake and heard the refrigerator door open. I waited for what I knew was coming.

"I thought I got two of these. What the—? Dev? Did you eat one of these caramel rolls?"

"I was starving, and they looked so good."

"We were going to share them and talk, remember? We agreed to have a conversation about our relationship this morning, where things are going. God."

"Well, this way, I won't be starving, and I'll be able to pay more attention to everything you say."

She gave me a long look, shook her head and muttered something, as she pulled a plate out of a kitchen cabinet and set it on the counter. She placed the caramel roll on the plate, then proceeded to cut it in half.

"Get your butt over here."

Thank God, she didn't say *'We need to talk'* because when a guy hears that, he automatically knows things just aren't going to go his way. I picked up my coffee mug and gave a last look out at the lake. The sun was up over the trees, and some sort of yellow bird, I think a goldfinch, was out on the deck flitting back and forth between two bird feeders. I gave the thing a longing look before I headed over to the kitchen counter, sat down on one of the wooden stools, took a deep breath, and braced myself.

Sophie pushed half of the caramel roll in front of me, topped up both our coffee mugs then took a sip. In the few short minutes she'd been in the living room, she had somehow loosened her silk dressing gown so it almost, but never quite revealed some of the attributes that kept me returning.

I took a sip of coffee, then reached for half of the caramel roll and said, "Okay, what's on your mind?"

"I really think we need to talk," she said.

Things went downhill from there.

Three

I somehow managed to escape Sophie's without being stabbed by a kitchen knife or getting doused with hot coffee. Just now, I was looking out my office window through binoculars, trying to catch sight of one of the women in the third-floor apartment across the street. I was beginning to think no one was home.

I watched as Louie pulled up across the street and waited for a car to park so he could back into the other open space. Louie was driving a blue Volkswagen Jetta. The thing was nothing if not boring. It was also nine years newer and a thousand times better than my 2003 Honda Accord. I already had the brakes replaced not once but twice, along with a new transmission last fall, but I digress.

I watched as Louie waited while the Mercedes backed into the parking spot then pulled ahead just enough to be perfectly positioned exactly in the middle of two parking spaces.

Louie apparently didn't honk, give the guy the finger or swear out the window like I would. Instead, he drove down to the far end of the block and grabbed a spot, not that the walk back wouldn't do him good.

I watched as a guy with a shaved head, mirrored sunglasses, and a grey strappy t-shirt climbed out of the Mercedes, pressed the lock button on his key fob, then hurried across the street and into our building. A moment later, I heard heavy footsteps coming up the stairs.

"You Haskell?" He said as he stood in the open doorway. He apparently didn't feel the need to take the sunglasses off. For some reason, I hadn't noticed it before, but there was a red cross on the front of his strappy t-shirt and below that the words *'Orgasm Donor'*. Morton got up and headed toward him, tail wagging. The guy shot a disapproving look in his direction, causing Morton to stop midway and hurry back to where he'd been sleeping in front of the file cabinet. He curled up on his pillow and sort of hid his face.

"You must be Ozzie Frick," I said, sounding more like an accusation than a question.

"Tubby filled you in?"

"No, not really, more like he said you had a problem, and you'd like me to take a look at it, but he didn't give me any specifics."

He sort of nodded and sat down in front of my desk. He pushed the stack of files at the edge of my desk toward the center, then tipped the client chair back and placed two cowboy boots on top of my desk. I'd been right all along. I wasn't going to like this guy.

"So, tell me about your problem."

"Nosey neighbor," he said.

"What?"

"Someone poking around into my private business."

"You talk to them?"

He half scoffed and shook his head. "We had words, didn't seem to do much good. I need her to back the hell off."

"What exactly is she doing?"

"Writing down the license numbers of my . . . customers. Anyone who stops in for a moment. She has a bullhorn, and she shouts their damn license number out, calls them all sorts of names, and then tells them she's calling the police."

"And are they doing anything illegal, or maybe the better question is, are you?"

He lowered his head and looked at me over the top of his mirrored sunglasses. "What I'm doing ain't the point here."

"It might be if she's calling the police. What did they say? Have you talked to them?"

"The cops? You gotta be kidding me. Did you listen to what I just said? She's taking down their license numbers and—"

"Yeah, I heard that part. Right off the top, it sounds like you're selling drugs or God knows what and no offense, but you gotta be nuts to think I'd help you with that sort of enterprise."

"But Tubby said you'd help."

I couldn't figure out if this Ozzie was really that stupid or if Tubby was setting me up. I thought about it for a half-second then said, "Tell you what, let me check into this. Where's this woman with the bullhorn live?"

He pulled an envelope from his pocket, unfolded it, and tossed the thing in my general direction. An address was scribbled across the back. "Here's her address. Her name is Debbie or Doris or something like that, don't know her last name. A real bitch. I tried to be nice once, but she wasn't having none of it. You're my last shot at being a good guy. You don't work out, all bets are off."

I could only imagine. Something wasn't right, and my first thought was *this woman was probably in more danger than she realized.* "I'll check her out this afternoon. For the time being, stay away from her. Let me check and see what, if anything, she's reported to the police."

"You'll keep me posted?" he said, slowly pulling his cowboy boots off my desk then groaning as he stood up.

I heard the building door close downstairs on the first floor, and then a familiar wheeze as Louie slowly made his way up the stairs.

"I need to have this dealt with right quick. Tubby said, you're the man."

"I'll see what I can do," I said, just as red-faced Louie stumbled into the office.

"Appreciate it. By the way, Tubby said this would be a freebie, said you owed him, big time."

Louie's eyes grew wide when Ozzie turned, gave him a nod, and headed out the door. Ozzie was out of the building and waiting for a bus to pass so he could cross the street before Louie was able to talk.

"That, that's the bastard that took up two parking places. I had to park about a mile away. I wasn't sure I was gonna be able to make it back to the office."

"Yeah, I know I was watching it out the window," I said and picked up the binoculars. I focused on Ozzie's license plate. It was from Illinois, and I wrote down the number. "If you hurry, you can see him getting back into that Mercedes. That space is going to be open. You could get back in your car and grab it."

Louie flopped into the chair behind the picnic table he used as a desk and loosened his tie. "If I never saw that parking hog again, it would be too soon. What was he doing up here?"

"Tubby Gustafson sent him."

"Tubby? Since when has anything he's been involved with ever worked out well for you?"

"Believe me, don't I know, and Tubby told him I'd help for free. God. That jerk. His name's Ozzie Frick, has a beef with a neighbor who's taking down license numbers and yelling over a bull horn at the people that are coming to see him."

"What?"

"Yeah. She sounds like an irate neighbor who's probably not too happy with that jackass selling drugs near her home."

"Figures he'd be involved in something like that. Gee, imagine. What do they hope to get from you?"

"That's the part that isn't making any sense. I'm going to go see her and if nothing else warn her and suggest she might want to be in touch with the police if she hasn't been already. It sounds like the screwiest damn thing. I can't quite figure out what Tubby's angle is in this."

Four

The address was over on the east side of town. An area that had experienced more than it's fair share of problems over the past fifty years. Like so many sections of town, there was a steady decline as manufacturing pulled out, housing prices fell. What had once been a strong working-class area was gradually carved up and whittled away. Shops along the main arteries began to close, single-family homes were broken up into multiple units, and opportunity seemed to disappear.

The address Ozzie had given me was on a dead-end street, six doors from a railroad line that, for all practical purposes, was now dormant. The factories the area had once served had already been gone for more than a quarter of a century.

The homes along the street were probably a century old, built just before or after the First World War. I guessed at least half of them were multiple units, everything from a duplex to five or six small efficiencies based on the mailboxes attached to the front of the houses. The address I'd been given appeared to still be a single-family home. The grass was cut, and a hedge along the front porch appeared neatly trimmed. The house looked freshly painted. The lapped wood siding was green with cream-colored trim and sort of a dark red accent color. The double front doors were painted black, and each had a panel of beveled glass. Three wooden steps led up to the front porch. A porch swing hung on the far end of the porch, and a woman who looked to be maybe sixtyish was sitting on the swing. I pulled over and parked.

My Honda Accord sort of groaned and sputtered for about ten seconds before shutting down completely. As I climbed out, I was aware she was watching me. I smiled and nodded as I stepped onto the sidewalk, but the moment I began to head onto her property, a vicious, deep-throated growl erupted from the porch, and some sort of wild-eyed animal was suddenly straining at a chain in an effort to get to me.

"I'd say you've gone just about far enough. What do you want?"

"I'm looking for Debbie or Doris, not sure which it is."

"It's Daisy, and this is my house, so what do you want?"

"I'd like to talk to you if I could," I had to raise my voice to be heard over the continuous barking and growling.

"I ain't the least bit interested in whatever it is you're selling if that's what this is all about."

"No ma'am, nothing like that. I, umm, understand you might be dealing with a problem at the end of your block." I nodded toward the dead end.

She seemed to eye me cautiously for a moment then said, "Axel, enough," and the dog immediately stopped barking. "Who told you that?"

"Neighborhood gossip. I just wanted to warn you. I don't think you're dealing with some very nice people."

"You threatening me?" Suddenly there was an edge to her voice. Axel, the dog, raised his head and seemed to take a renewed interest in me.

"No ma'am, I would just suggest that you be careful, maybe contact the police if you haven't yet. If you're taking down makes of cars, license numbers, and maybe the times those cars are here, you should give the cops that information. Sometimes it takes a while, but if you can establish a pattern, it can help them in shutting things down."

"What's your name?"

"Haskell, Dev Haskell. Actually, I'm a private investigator, so I deal with the police a good bit of the time."

"Maybe you'd like to come up on the porch, so we're not having to yell back and forth."

"Is your dog going to be okay with that?"

"Axel? He'll get used to you, just don't move too fast and you should be okay. His bark is worse than his bite."

Not exactly encouraging. I took two or three tentative steps toward the porch and heard the links on Axel's chain suddenly drag across the wooden porch floor. He waited at the top step, eyes flared, and teeth showing. He growled and dared me to step onto the front porch.

"That's just his way of saying hello," she said. "Now Axel, you be nice, don't bite. You know I don't like that."

Axel took a step toward me, bared his teeth again and barked some more.

"Maybe if I just stayed down here, we could talk."

"Don't be silly. He just wants to let you know he's doing his job."

"Yeah, not to worry, I got that message loud and clear."

"Axel, get back here," she said and yanked on the heavy chain connected to his choke collar. "Come on, come on, Axel, you get back here."

He seemed to grudgingly give way, as I cautiously climbed up the front steps.

"Come on up, Mr. Hassle. I'd say he likes you."

"Oh great, I'd hate to see him when he didn't."

Axel was at her feet now, watching my every move, teeth bared and still growling. At least he wasn't barking and lurching toward me.

"Please, take a seat," she said, pointing to a pressed-back wooden chair that looked like it might have been original to the house.

I could feel the sweat in my armpits and a long drop running down my back. I smiled at Axel, being sure not to show any teeth.

His growl turned deeper, no doubt he sensed my fear.

"I think he likes you."

"I'd hate to see him mad," I said and tried to ignore the growls.

Five

I'd been on the porch for the better part of an hour. At the moment, Daisy was on her feet, writing down the license number and description of the latest car that headed toward the end of the block. That gave me a chance to sneak another peanut butter cookie to Axel from the plate Daisy had brought out.

"I don't know," she said, shaking her head and sitting back down on the porch swing. "You'd think they'd be smart enough to know whatever it is he's selling isn't going to be good for them."

"I think you're giving them too much credit," I said.

"They just don't seem to care. That's the third car since you arrived, and it's not even the busiest time."

"When is it the busiest?"

"Oh, maybe from about ten until one in the morning, then it stops for maybe forty-five minutes before things pick up again from two to three in the morning."

"In the morning?"

She nodded just as Axel placed a sloppy, wet tennis ball on my khaki slacks.

"Oh, I'd say you've made a friend."

I looked at the muddy stain on my leg. I guess it was better than being chewed on.

"You worried about threats from anyone? Your safety? It's not like you're dealing with well balanced, responsible individuals."

"That's why I have Axel."

"But these idiots are quite capable of driving by and shooting you or setting your house on fire in the middle of the night. It's not clear to me why you don't contact the police."

"I've been in touch with them from time to time, and they make the occasional drive past to make sure I'm all right."

"Yeah, but they can't be here all the time and that idiot Ozzie, I mean, he's liable to lose it some time and go right off the deep end."

"I'm not afraid of him."

"My first impression was he's not the brightest bulb on the tree. You should be careful."

"But I am, that's why I have Axel," she said, just as Axel dropped the tennis ball on my khaki pants again. I took the ball and rolled it along the length of the porch. Axel dragged his chain after it.

"What can I do to help you?"

"Oh, that's very kind of you to offer, but I'm really quite all right. Besides, I have a plan."

"A plan?"

She nodded but didn't say anything else.

“I’ve got some friends on the police force, Daisy. I can get in touch with them and maybe get something going.”

“Oh, no, don’t do that. Like I said, I’m in touch with the police. I’m keeping an eye out, making a note of the activity as it comes and goes, and besides, I’ve got you’re new best friend, Axel.”

“Yeah, Axel,” I said, then caught the tennis ball before he dropped it in my lap again. I rolled it down the length of the porch one more time then stood, brushing cookie crumbs onto the porch floor. “Well, you’ve got my number. If you need anything, just call. If it’s okay, I may just swing by every now and then just to check in on you and Axel. Make sure everything is okay.”

“That would be nice. It was a pleasure meeting you, Mr. Hassle, feel free to stop by anytime.”

“Please, call me, Dev,” I said, then picked up the tennis ball Axel had laid at my feet and rolled it back down the length of the porch. “Thanks for the cookies.”

“I’m sure Axel liked his, too,” she said and smiled.

Six

I've got a friend who's a cop, a number of friends actually. I drove straight from Daisy's house to the main police station in town, pulled into the parking lot then hurried across the street.

"I'd like to see Lieutenant Aaron LaZelle, in homicide," I said to the desk sergeant. She was a woman who looked to be in her mid to late thirties with dark hair pulled back in a bun just like Sophie had this morning. Her name tag read, Perez, M. She seemed a little on the petite side from what I thought a sergeant on the police force should be.

"Is he expecting you?"

"No, not exactly, but I think I have some information on a potential homicide."

"You?"

"No, it's just a situation I'd like to make him aware of, warn him about it before anything happens."

"Let me see if one of our patrols might be better able to help you out. Where, exactly, is this going to—"

"Would you just give Lieutenant LaZelle a call, my name is Dev Haskell, and I've worked with him over a number of years."

"I really think a patrol might be—"

"Look, sorry to have wasted your time, Sergeant. I'll just call him myself and talk to him."

"Hold on. I'll try him," she said, giving me a look before punching in a couple of numbers on her keyboard then adjusting her headphone. "They're pretty busy up there, and I don't know if they . . .

"Yes, Lieutenant, sorry to bother you. I have a gentleman down here with information regarding a potential homicide. A Mr. Haskell. He . . . Yes, Sir, he is. No, he did not. No Sir, I haven't given him a breathalyzer. Yes, Sir, right in front of me. All right, thank you, I'll let him know."

"So?" I said once she hung up and looked at me.

"He thinks you've probably been drinking, but he'll see you anyway. He's sending someone down."

"Okay, thanks."

"Might be a couple of minutes, maybe just grab a chair over there. I'll call you when someone comes down."

I nodded then sat down in an uncomfortable plastic chair against the far wall. There was a dogeared Field & Stream magazine from February of 2014 lying on the chair next to me. The address label in the lower right hand corner had been torn off, suggesting it was maybe a personal subscription someone had been kind enough to leave behind. The cover featured the picture of a twelve-point buck and the copy, 18 True Tales of America's Favorite Hunt. I'd barely gotten into the third paragraph when desk Sergeant, Perez, called out, "Mr. Haskell?"

I tossed the Field & Stream back onto the chair where I'd found it, then hurried up to the desk. Perez flashed a stunning smile of gorgeous white teeth. "The detective will escort you up," she said, then nodded toward a partially open door.

Someone seemed to be involved in a conversation behind the door. I couldn't quite make out what was being said, although the voice sounded familiar. I headed towards the door then slowed my pace considerably as the conversation stopped, and the door opened wide.

"Mr. Haskell, what a surprise. How nice of you to turn yourself in and save us the trouble of sending a squad car." Detective Norris Manning, never a fan of mine. The feeling was mutual because I certainly didn't like him. He had cold blue eyes and a bald head that at the moment was pale pink, although I'd seen it go crimson on more than one occasion. He cracked the always present piece of gum between his teeth and set his unsmiling focus on me.

"Detective Manning, I hope all's well with you," I said, trying to get things off on the right foot.

He grunted, held the door as I stepped inside, then hurried past me and pressed the elevator button. The elevator door opened a moment later. There was no romance to the elevator. If you were in an office building, it might have had wood panels on the walls or maybe boring beige colored walls. I've been in some fancy ones with beveled mirrors and once, in a building of million-dollar condos, red velvet paneled walls.

This elevator was more of a freight elevator with the occasional dent in the wall just below the six-foot mark where some poor slob had gotten his head bounced off the wall.

"Kidnapping and murder of an elderly couple?" Manning asked.

"What?"

"Abduction of an underage girl?"

"What do you mean?"

"Drowning of a pregnant woman?"

"What the hell are you going on about, Manning?"

"I'm wondering why you're here. Don't get me wrong. I'm thrilled you're finally ready to confess. Believe me. We're all thrilled. I'm just wondering what you're actually going to confess to. You know, if you wanted to tell me now, I could get things going. Put it on the fast track, eliminate a lot of hassle and work for all involved, even yourself. We could have you on death row by the end of the day."

"Nice try, but there's no death penalty in Minnesota."

He nodded, "Yeah, but we could make an exception. In your case, I'm sure it would sail right through to the Federal level."

"Gee, thanks. Glad you have my best interests at heart."

The elevator door opened, and Manning stepped out, then turned and looked at me, "Coming?"

"I suddenly wasn't all that sure where he was going to take me."

"Lieutenant LaZelle is here, right?"

"If you say so," Manning said, then headed off down the hall. Against my better judgment I followed. Manning headed around a corner then down a hall toward where the interview rooms were located, just another name for interrogation. I figured it would be just like him to place me in one of those rooms, then conveniently forget that I was in there and leave me sitting for four or five hours.

"Oh, Dev, there you are. What are you doing back here? Come on down to my office?" Aaron called from down the hall. He had the sleeves on his shirt rolled up to his elbows, his tie was undone, and he carried what looked like a half-dozen files in one hand and a coffee cup in the other.

At the sound of Aaron's voice, Manning turned around with a disappointed look on his face.

"Manning was just escorting me," I said.

"Well, quit screwing around and come into my office, you want a coffee?"

"From your machine up here, ahh, no, thanks."

"Come on. Actually, glad you stopped by. I got a question for you."

Seven

Aaron shook his head and said, "Oh, man, I tell you, if I have to attend another budget meeting anytime soon, I think I'm going to jump out the nearest window." He set the stack of files he carried on the credenza behind his desk. He drained the paper coffee cup, grimaced as he swallowed, then dropped the cup in a wastepaper basket and sat down behind his desk.

"A budget meeting?" I said. "Who did you piss off to have to go to a budget meeting? Sounds dreadful."

"Yeah, you don't know the half of it. We're supposed to add thirty officers next year and still cut everything by seven percent. Let me know if you can come up with a way that's going to work. But enough of my headaches, what the hell do you want? Like the day hasn't been bad enough already."

"I can tell you in two words. Tubby Gustafson."

"Oh, shit. What's he up to now?"

I told Aaron my story of Tubby pulling me out of The Spot, leaving me in the reclusive parking area on the River Boulevard after telling me in so many words that Daisy was interfering with his business just a few doors down. I didn't mention the fact that I was late getting over to my friend Sophie's, and she wasn't all that happy by the time I arrived at her place. To say that the night's mood had been ruined was a bit of an understatement.

"Okay, so two questions, is this the same scenic parking area where you drank all the root beer flavored schnapps when we were kids? And come on, what was the girl's name?" Aaron said, snapping his fingers. "Help me out here, Dev."

"It's not important."

"Relax, I'm sure she thanks her lucky stars she didn't end up with you. Come on, what was her name?"

"Jackie Donnelly."

"Yeah, that's the one. Jackie. Didn't she go on to be a model or something?"

"She was in Playboy when they did that series on college girls. Then she modeled for Vogue for a bit. She finally settled somewhere in Europe in the last few years, France or someplace. She's a big name in the fashion industry. I think she has her own brand name."

"You ever link up with her again. I mean, she was hot."

"No. But then, you already knew that. Remember, she sent me that letter that she never wanted anything to do with me ever again? She started that club in high school of girls who vowed they'd never go out with me."

"That was her? I thought that was Karen Nilsson. She really didn't like you."

"Well yeah, it was her too, the two of them. They sort of formed that club together, if you'll recall, they had their own lunch table, and then they made that dartboard with a picture of me."

"It grew to be more than just one table. If I recall, wasn't it all the cheerleaders and the girls' soccer team for starters."

"Could we maybe move on from the ancient history lesson and just get back to the reason I'm here, what I witnessed and the problem as I see it."

"Sure, go ahead."

"So, like I was saying, Tubby Gustafson has a friend who is being harassed by this woman. In actuality, she's documenting people showing up at this idiot's house, apparently buying drugs. She's got car descriptions, license plate numbers, along with dates and times. I saw three different vehicles there in the middle of the day. There's some idiot out front of the place who takes the cash. The buyer waits in the car then leaves when he gets what he wants. Apparently, he's doing a hell of a night-time business until about two in the morning. Aside from the obvious problems, my concern is if Tubby mentioned her to me, he's looking for a way to eliminate this headache."

"The neighbor lady."

"Yeah, exactly. I tried to caution her. Told her to get in touch with the police, but you know the drill. She was going to handle it her way. Like yelling on a bullhorn is going to intimidate some idiot out to make a drug buy."

"If she's got Tubby's attention, she's already on thin ice," Aaron said.

"It strikes me as a given whoever that idiot is selling, he's ultimately working for Tubby. If you guys raid the place, you could shut him down, probably make some low-level arrests, but more importantly, save this woman's life."

"This Daisy person."

"Aaron, she's doing the upstanding citizen gig, and she's got no idea the type of trouble she's courting."

"Let me get Nelson up here. You got some time to go over this with him?"

"Yeah, I suppose. He's with narcotics?"

"Yeah, heads up the unit. Let me see if he's in," he said and picked up the phone.

Eight

Gary Nelson was a large guy with close-cropped blonde hair and green eyes. He looked like he would have played high school and maybe college football. Based on the physical shape he appeared to be in, he could have suited up this afternoon and started in a game.

He nodded as I retold my story, suggesting he was familiar with the situation then said, "This place is at the end of the street, right? The street dead-ends at some railroad tracks?"

"Yeah, a white house with a front porch on sort of a hill. There's a cul-de-sac at the end of the street, makes it easy for these folks to place their order, pay up, then turn around while they're waiting for delivery."

"Familiar with it," he said.

"Familiar with it? Why haven't you shut it down?"

"We were hoping to get someone just a little higher up than some deadbeat working street traffic."

"Ozzie Frick is there, would that make it worth your while?"

"Ozzie's barely middle management."

"Well, both he and Tubby Gustafson suggested they have plans to deal with their problem three doors down. So, I'd say he's on the way up in Tubby's organization. Far as I can tell, this Daisy is the only person standing up to Ozzie Frick. She's sort of like the Lone Ranger trying to save the last vestige of what was once a solid neighborhood. She's got documentation of everything that's been going on there, license numbers, times, descriptions. I mean these people making the buys are so brazen she's yelling at 'em on a bullhorn, and they just sit there in their car and wait for the delivery. Obviously, they aren't worried about anything happening to them. She said, sometimes they drive off and give her a friendly wave, maybe even toot their horn. Something bad happens to her, I gotta tell you guys, you're gonna have a real public relations nightmare on your hands."

"You said Tubby Gustafson wanted you to deal with this problem?"

"More like, if I don't, *he will* type of thing. She's a tough old bird, but I think she's kind of naive when you're dealing with someone the likes of Tubby. He'll just have her hauled away, and they'll find her floating ten miles downriver, and I might end up right next to her."

"What's your relationship with Tubby?" Nelson asked.

"He's been working with us for years where Tubby's involved," Aaron said. "He's been a good source in the past, Gary."

"I gotta be honest, I'm not doubting what you say, Haskell, but our information suggests that site is not a Tubby enterprise. First of all, he's a hell of a lot smarter than that. His M.O. doesn't include waving it in our face. This Ozzie Frick, he's nothing short of a Neanderthal. If he has a couple of bad nights, he's liable to go down to this woman's house and just start shooting."

"Well, if it's not one of Tubby's, whose is it?"

"Information we have is Dwyer," Nelson said.

"Curtis Dwyer?" I said. "I thought he was locked up?"

"He is, we think this is his kid, Dennis trying to run things."

"Dennis Dwyer? I thought he was some high rolling attorney, threatening small businesses with handicap access lawsuits."

"Yeah, among other things."

I pondered that for a long moment, then said, "In a way, you seem to have painted an even grimmer picture than the one I had. But if this is a Dwyer operation, why is Tubby Gustafson involved?"

"One of many questions," Nelson said. "Did Tubby suggest any sort of time frame to you?"

"Not in so many words, but he sort of left me with the thought that sooner rather than later would be a good idea."

"Let's just say we raid the place, shut it down, arrest Ozzie, and whatever scumbags we can get there. What sort of position would that put you in?"

"Me?" I had to think for a moment. "Tubby might be pissed off, maybe, but as long as they don't actually see me there, I'll be okay. It's still not making sense. If it's a Dwyer operation, you'd think Tubby would jump at the chance to see the thing shut down."

Nelson drummed his index finger on the arm of the chair. "You know, I'm thinking we can do a couple of things. Bring some equipment out, park it there, make it look like street repair. That'll cut down on the immediate traffic. Then we can set up a post to film activity." Nelson had his eyes raised, clearly thinking. "Let me check out a couple of things, not the least is why we don't have this place listed to Tubby. I'll keep you posted. You willing to lend a hand if we need it?"

"Me?" I said. "Yeah, sure, I guess. I just don't want to see anything happening to this upstanding citizen, Daisy, she's my main concern."

"Let me get on this, I got some ideas," Nelson said but didn't elaborate.

Nine

Sophie said, "No, no, it's not that, I really like it, in fact, I love the stuff. Shrimp and garlic, you know it's one of my favorites. I'm just amazed you didn't bring rare steaks, still bleeding, with onion rings and a half case of red wine so I won't know my own name by bedtime."

"Your talk the other morning helped me to show my caring, sensitive side," I said, hoping we could skip another *'We have to talk'* conversation and just get down to the physical aspects of our relationship.

"Who knew you had a caring, sensitive side, Dev," she said, but then laughed and gave me a kiss.

I'd recovered, mostly, from the *talk* we apparently needed to have. Nothing I hadn't heard before in a long list of past relationships. More involvement, sharing my feelings, some form of commitment, telling her about whatever case I was working on. It was like they all read the same article about how to take the excitement out of any night, at any time, anywhere.

When I attempted to mention a couple of things regarding Sophie's side of the relationship like her obsession with rules, dog behavior, and always mentioning the cost of things, she'd said, "We're not talking about that right now."

"So, we're just talking about what I've screwed up?"

"Yeah, and we don't have enough time," she'd said, and continued on from there.

So, I'd picked up two orders of shrimp and garlic from Carmelo's as a peace offering after the other night, along with the promise I'd be more caring and understanding, something I knew I was probably doomed to fail at but thought I might try, anyway.

It was raining out, which actually worked well for me. I didn't have to fool with a fire in her patio fire pit. We weren't going to take the boat out onto the lake, and about all that left us to do was enjoy the dinner, sip some wine and, hopefully, spend some time in bed before we both fell asleep.

Sophie was busy putting the shrimp and garlic onto her china plates while I opened the bottle of wine. The plates had an image of a chocolate Labrador on them. She loved the things, I thought they were really stupid.

"You want a glass?" I said, partially filling a glass.

She sort of gave me a strange look, then said, "Well, yeah."

"Okay, great. No pressure. I just didn't want you to think I was trying to get you drunk, you know, so we'd hop into bed."

"Not to worry, the dinner you brought will accomplish that. The wine is just the icing on the cake," she said and smiled. “But thanks for saying it anyway. Nice to know you actually listened to what I said the other night.”

Fortunately, I hadn’t been drinking. That was the sort of statement that could bring out a stupid comment from me, lead to an argument, and ruin the rest of the evening with both of us equally guilty. Instead, we just clinked glasses in a toast.

“Can I ask you something?”

“Of course, Dev, you can ask me anything.”

“I’m working on a case and I—”

“Are you kidding? Oh. My. God. I don’t believe it. You really did listen to me the other night.”

“I just wanted to get your opinion is all.”

“Ask away,” she said, leaning forward on the kitchen counter and giving me her undivided attention.

“Okay. So, I’m sort of working this case. It’s over on the east side town. A drug dealer seems to be operating out of this house that’s three doors down from a woman I met. Relax,” I said when she gave me the look. “She’s old enough to be my mother. She sits on her front porch and yells at people pulling up to make a buy.”

“You mean she’s screaming at them?”

“Sort of. She’s actually got a bullhorn that she uses to yell at them. She takes down the license number, the color and make of the car, and the time and date that they’re there.”

Sophie seemed to think about that for a moment, then said. “My first thought is given the nature of the people in the car. It probably represents what might be classed as not the greatest cross-section of society. There's a good chance they might be the sort of person who would retaliate, maybe violently. Then, if this neighbor of hers is selling drugs, I mean, doesn't that make him just a little more dangerous than the average idiot? I would think, in short order, he might do something stupid like burn her house down or attack her. Doesn't sound like the sort of neighbor you could have a conversation with to get your point across."

"Yeah, right in both cases."

"So, what's the problem?" Sophie said.

"I'm thinking of helping the police in their investigation."

"Hmm-mmm. Exactly what does, 'helping the police' really mean? Are you going to be peeking in windows or something?"

"Not exactly sure, but I know they're trying to work through budget cuts. The way this thing might shape up, they won't have the funds to provide any surveillance. I'm thinking, maybe I could do that, or help do it."

"And how, exactly, are you thinking you would do this? Hide in the weeds or up in a tree?"

"Maybe, I don't know yet, but it's something that might pop up. Maybe, just sit on the other side of these railroad tracks and, I don't know, watch, or something."

"Have they asked you?"

"No, not in so many words, we just had one early discussion. But one of the bad guys has given indications he's getting fed up with this woman yelling on the bull horn," I said, without mentioning Tubby by name.

"Did you tell the police?"

"Yeah, but they can't really do anything. He can pretty much say whatever he wants, last time I checked, we still had a semblance of free speech in the country. But this woman with the bullhorn has clearly gotten this guy's attention, and that probably isn't the best thing."

"And if you did this surveillance, would that provide the police with enough information to act? To arrest this creep selling drugs?"

"It might. More likely, it would just serve as a start. I mean, to tell the truth, I could sit there for a month, and at the end of it wouldn't have much more information than what we have now."

"A start, what exactly does that mean?"

"Meaning, I'm not exactly sure what it means. If you're thinking I would watch the place for a night and then the cops would swoop in and arrest people, it doesn't really work like that. They, the cops, would like to get something besides two or three people in a car and some idiot lingering in the bushes. Ideally, they'd nail the guy who owns the house, a jerk named Ozzie, and get him to give up the name of his supplier, move up the chain."

"Oh, kind of like on TV."

"I guess I never thought of it quite like that, but yeah."

"How long do you think this would be? Two nights? A week?"

"I don't really know, could be a few nights, a month, or months. I just don't know, and I'm not even sure they're going to do anything. They said they'd look into it, but it's probably one of dozens of places they're taking a look at."

"You know, Dev. I kind of think I liked it better when I wasn't involved in some of what happens in your job. How about some shrimp and garlic, and it might be a good idea if you topped off my wine glass?"

I topped off her wine glass then placed the pasta bowls on the kitchen counter. Sophie quickly changed the subject to looking for a breeder to mate with Lilly. Then waxed eloquent for the next three hours on the benefits of purebred, show winning dogs, and the amount she could make selling the puppies. It all sounded like way too much work to me.

Ten

Sophie had the air conditioning on, so she was under a sheet and a blanket, sound asleep, and breathing deeply. We'd had a great dinner and too much wine, which led to Sophie telling me she'd *'catch me in the morning'* just before she fell asleep. Now, I was wide awake, worrying about what was going to happen to Daisy. It wasn't so much Tubby that concerned me, but Ozzie Frick struck me as a real loose cannon, capable of all sorts of stupid reactions.

I groaned a few times and rolled back and forth, tugged on the sheet and blanket, all to no avail. She remained sound asleep. After about twenty minutes of trying to wake her, I quietly slid out of bed, headed to the kitchen and put on the coffee.

Sophie's dog Lilly was curled up in her bed in the kitchen. She slowly opened one eye, then snuggled down and dropped back to sleep. I guess that was a good indication she was getting used to me. I pulled the pot from the coffee maker as soon as the first cup had been brewed, filled my cup, then headed into the living room and settled onto the couch to stare absently out at the lake.

I kept thinking about Daisy and what I could possibly do to help. Gary Nelson, the narcotics cop, seemed to be the key on that end, although the budget cuts had me worried. If I couldn't get Gary involved, I figured I could maybe go back to Daisy and monitor evening activity from her front porch. Hopefully, stop her from yelling at people with the bullhorn, just for her own protection. That might give me the chance to tell Tubby I was keeping her quiet and stop him, or more likely, stop Ozzie Frick from doing something stupid.

I kept thinking about Nelson telling me Ozzie was barely middle management, and they were looking for a bigger target. That suggested to me they might have their sights set on Tubby, and I couldn't shake the idea that selling drugs out of that house seemed way too small time for Tubby. Not to mention the fact that Nelson had suggested he thought Dennis Dwyer was the guy ultimately running this operation.

I drained my mug and was about to get up for a refill when I saw someone just offshore. I sort of shook my head and blinked a couple of times. A figure walking on water? With a red nose and clown makeup? I sniffed my mug, trying to detect the scent of something besides coffee. Nothing.

I looked out at the lake again. Now, all I could see was early morning fog. The sun would probably be over the trees in the next fifteen minutes and burn it off. I shook my head, figured I was losing what was left of my mind then wandered back into the kitchen for a coffee refill.

Sophie was up an hour later. She walked into the kitchen without saying anything, then came back with a mug of coffee and settled into the opposite end of the couch.

"You up long?"

"Couple of hours. No reflection on you. What are you doing with the rest of your day?"

"I've got a late lunch with B.B., one of my neighborhood pals. She's looking for a new outfit, and we're going shopping at the Mall. Want to come?"

I couldn't tell if she was kidding so I quickly changed the subject. "Hey, nice to chat last night," I lied. "Thanks for letting me bounce some ideas off you."

"Yeah, it was good, wasn't it? I told you shrimp and garlic is one of my favorites."

I looked over at her and sort of sighed, hoping she'd remember about *catching me in the morning*. No such luck. "Well, I suppose . . ." I said, waiting for her to pick up on the hint.

She didn't. "Hey, thanks for sharing your work stuff. Not sure I wanted to hear about it, but thank you for including me. I need to know these things."

"I've been up trying to figure out a fallback plan, in case the cops don't have the budget or can't see a result that would be worth the effort. I'm not having much luck coming up with anything, thus far."

"Something will turn up, it always does."

I sort of shook my head.

"What?" she said.

"You're going to think I'm nuts."

"Dev, I thought that from the first night we met at the dog obedience class. So, we're way past that point. What is it?"

"Humph. Okay, so, I'm sitting here staring out the window, trying to figure out how I can help this woman and I'm just looking out at the lake when I see—"

"The clown. Oh. My. God. I don't believe it. You actually saw him?"

"How in the hell did you know that?" I said.

"The clown? People have been seeing him for years. Supposedly, some guy even took a video of him one time. I think it's on YouTube. I looked at it once, but it didn't make any sense. But if you Google the name of the lake—"

"Alimagnet?"

"Yeah, all sorts of links come up with the ghost clown."

"I've never heard of it before."

"Kind of surprised you saw him. Usually the sightings are around dusk."

"You don't think I'm crazy?"

"I maybe wouldn't go that far, Dev. I just said I believe you when you say you saw the clown. What was he doing?"

"Doing? It was just sort of there, kind of half floating out there in the fog. I blinked my eyes a couple of times, and it was gone. But I swear I saw the thing."

"I believe you, baby. Hey, you're like one of the locals now. God, I'll have to call the girls and let them know."

"Maybe hold off on that for a while. Not exactly the kind of information I want out there."

"Okay. Just saying, I believe you. Another coffee?"

"You know, no, thanks, I better take a pass. I should get back to the safety of the inner city. I have to check on Morton, and I want to see if the cops made any sort of decision."

"Thanks for the shrimp and garlic, it was really good."

Yeah, unfortunately, it was obvious nothing was going to happen.

Eleven

We'd just turned the corner and were in sight of the house, Morton and I, finishing up our morning walk, when my cellphone rang. I didn't recognize the number.

"Haskell investigations."

"Haskell, Gary Nelson, you got a minute?"

"Yeah, go ahead, actually I was just getting ready to give you a call. What's the news?"

"Well, good and not so good. But, let me explain and let's see if you can give us a hand. We mentioned we're working under the budget ax, and we're also attempting to add thirty more officers department-wide next year."

"Yeah. I gotta tell you, just as an outsider and a city resident, it sounds like mission impossible."

"Not far from the truth, but here's the good news. We're thinking we could set up a construction site out on that cul-de-sac."

"A construction site? Out in front of Ozzie Frick's place. What would you be building?"

"Not building, but road construction. Make it look like we're going to resurface the road. We wouldn't necessarily set up in front because that would eliminate any traffic coming in and going out, which would sort of defeat the purpose. So, I'm thinking, we set up along the property that's basically along the curb of the cul-de-sac, technically it would be railroad property."

"When would you do this?"

"Today, as a matter of fact, they'll be moving things into position later this afternoon. We've got the city's help in parking some equipment there that'll at least give us the look of a repair project."

"Okay, so far, so good. So what's the bad news?"

"Manpower. I can only staff it for twelve hours. That's if I can con some volunteer time from folks."

"Twelve hours?"

"Yeah, basically a daytime shift, one and a half people from roughly eight to five."

"What? You gotta be kidding."

"Two people, one at eight hours and another at four hours. Here's the thing, it's going to immediately raise questions if my team is there after hours. Other than maybe freeway or bridge work, when was the last time you saw folks doing road work in the evening? Especially on a dead-end street?"

"But that's the busiest time, after dark. Hell, after midnight is probably the highest volume traffic. Folks out on the town, feeling no pain, making dumb decisions, and they show up to buy."

"I know, I know, that's where I was thinking you might come in."

"How? What difference does it make if it's me or one of your guys? We're all going to look out of place."

"Only if they see you."

"Bad idea, if you want me hiding in some hole in the ground."

"Relax, we've got something lined up that will keep you dry and comfortable, complete with recording equipment and high def radio contact. It would probably be one of the most comfortable night time gigs you've ever had."

"Some sort of truck parked on-site?"

"Even better."

I thought about that for a moment then figured if I could do something to take the pressure off of Daisy before Ozzie Frick blew a gasket, it would be worth it. "Okay, I'm in. When do I start?"

"What's your schedule like tonight?"

I had nothing going, other than taking Morton for another walk. "Tonight? Kind of jammed, but let me make some calls. I think once I explain things, I can clear my calendar and move this to the top of the client list. I, umm, hesitate to ask about remuneration."

"Oh, yeah, ahh, we're working on that. Kind of a dicey deal, as you can probably imagine. Since you're not actually in the department or anything, we're kind of walking a fine line. But we'll figure something out and make sure you get taken care of. Sound like a plan?"

"I'll hold you to that, tell me where and when and I'll be there."

"Come on down to the station, say three o'clock this afternoon. We'll give you the layout, what you'll be dealing with, and we'll transport you to the site. Okay?"

"Yeah, okay. I'll see you in your office this afternoon," I said.

"Okay, three o'clock, and I'll give you an overview. It will give you the opportunity to meet the other guys," he said, then disconnected.

Twelve

Aaron LaZelle met me in the lobby and then brought me up to Gary Nelson's office. Once we stepped onto the elevator, and the doors closed, he said, "Here's the deal, Dev. We've kept things kind of quiet, as far as bringing you on board. So, anyone asks, just don't say anything. Okay?"

"Yeah, okay. But just for my own information, what exactly do you mean by kind of quiet?"

"Well, exactly that, no one knows you're going to be there tonight."

"What about tomorrow night or the night after that?"

"Same deal, no one knows you're going to be there."

"Sounds like the sort of thing you could lose your job over."

"Don't limit it to just me. Everyone is a volunteer on this operation. Devitt and Wilkes, you're going to meet them in just a couple of minutes, they're working this on their own time, off the books, they aren't getting paid."

"No offense, but why are you guys doing this? It can't be because of Daisy yelling at people on her bullhorn."

"Let's just say it's an opportunity for us to make a big score, nail a scumbag who, up until now, has been next to impossible to get. Things work out, we can eliminate a major player in the game, at least for a while, until the next one comes along. More importantly, with these budget cuts staring us in the face, a big score right now might go a long way to reminding folks what's at stake."

"But Nelson said Ozzie Frick was barely middle management."

"That's still the case. Ozzie Frick is just a stepping stone, but with a little pressure, we think we can turn him so he'll see the light."

The elevator doors opened, and I followed Aaron out and down the hall.

Gary Nelson's office was similar to Aaron's and looked like a 50's movie set. Nelson was confined to a glass-walled corner affair with dusty white Venetian blinds covering the windows that looked out into a room of ancient wooden desks pushed together.

Three worn chairs sat on the opposite side of Nelson's desk. The desk itself was buried somewhere beneath stacks of files, with more files piled up against a far wall. The detectives at the desks were kind of sketchy looking guys with beards, earrings, a couple of ponytails, and one large nose ring, but then again, that was the world they were working in.

The door to Gary Nelson's office was open, and Aaron knocked on the doorframe as he stepped in. Nelson was on the phone with his back to the door, and he spun around in his desk chair when Aaron knocked. He nodded and pointed to the chairs in front of his desk. All three had a stack of files resting on them. Nelson continued with his phone conversation, as we took the files from two chairs and set them on the floor against the side of the desk.

"No, that's not going to work. We need to nail him with the cash in his possession. You've got the serial number? Okay, great, once you bring him in, we'll just let him cool his heels in the interview room. He can think about the limited options he'll be facing, maybe decide it would make more sense to work with us. Yeah, I know, I know, but that's all we can offer. Good luck, see you when you get here," he said, then hung up.

"Aaron, you bring him up to speed?" he said and nodded at me.

"As much as possible, you can never really tell if he understands what he's being told or if it's going completely over his head."

"Thanks for the vote of confidence," I said. "Yeah, I get it, this is basically off the books. Right?"

"I've no idea what you're talking about," Nelson said.

There was a knock on the door frame, and I turned around to look at two guys as they stepped into the already crowded office. They were dressed in jeans and t-shirts and had high visibility green vests over their t-shirts. Both of them carried yellow hard hats under their arms. They looked like what they were supposed to be, construction guys.

"How'd it go?" Nelson said.

"Perfect, we've got everything set up. Communications check passed with flying colors. The office is padlocked," he said, setting a brass key on one of the stacks of files on Nelson's desk.

"Office?" I said.

"Have you two met P.I. Haskell yet? He's volunteered to take the night shift for us. Haskell, meet the infamous Detective's Devitt and Wilkes."

We shook hands and nodded at one another.

"Yeah, weren't you the one who said you didn't want to spend the night sitting in a hole in the ground?"

"Well, yeah, but an office? I can do that. This sounds like it's going to be a piece of cake."

Wilkes and Devitt seemed to exchange a look then smiled at one another.

"Yeah, it took some doing, but with a little groveling we were able to get a portable office onto the site, make sure you'd be nice and comfortable over the course of the night," Wilkes said.

"Yeah, it was the least we could do, you volunteering your time and all. Might as well be comfortable, don't you think?" Devitt added.

"It's not that large, but then again, it'll just be you, so all you really have to do is sit there and watch the monitor. You'll be able to record anyone who comes and goes with the press of a button."

"I think I can handle that."

"The structure is pretty standard. Once you see it, I'm sure you've been in an office like this before."

"You'll know you're way around after just a few seconds," Wilkes said.

"Questions?" Nelson said.

I shook my head, no.

"We'll take you back over there. The key is going to be for you to casually slip into the office. We'll hang around for another fifteen minutes or so, then leave. Once you're in the office, you're going to have to stay there until we show up again tomorrow morning. That going to work for you?"

"Shouldn't be a problem," I said.

"Well, then, we'll leave you to it," Nelson said.

"You take care of yourself, Dev, and thank you for volunteering," Aaron said.

Thirteen

Wilkes and Devitt seemed to be nice enough guys, and we chatted about everything and nothing on the way back over to the east side, Wilkes was driving. We were traveling in a white van with yellow flashing lights mounted onto the roof. A Department of Public Works logo was painted on the doors. They even stopped at a McDonalds and bought me a couple of Double Cheeseburgers, fries, and a strawberry shake for my dinner.

"Hey, guys, you didn't have to do this, really," I said.

"You kidding, you're gonna be there all night, it seems like the least we can do," Wilkes said.

"Yeah, and you volunteered. No point in having to starve yourself on top of it," Devitt said.

When we were about a half-mile from Daisy's street, Wilkes said, "There was virtually no activity while we were there earlier today, but that's only because this was day one. After a couple of days, people will get used to our set up there, and the traffic is bound to return to normal."

"A few days?" Devitt said and scoffed. "Traffic'll be back tonight. Like we said earlier, we're going to drop you off, hang around pretending we're busy for fifteen or twenty minutes, then head out. Soon as we get there you can just head into the office. It's a blue structure, can't miss it. No one will ever know you're still in there by the time we leave. One of the things we're looking for is product delivery and maybe the cash pickup."

"Cash pickup?"

"Whoever is running this operation, they aren't trusting idiot Ozzie with the night's receipts. He's strictly entry-level, trying to work his way up. Trouble is, he's a bigger numbskull than the rest of them. Anyway, look for some kind of pickup vehicle toward the end of the night," Wilkes said.

"You got any questions before we drop you off?"

"No, sounds simple enough. You said the communications check went all right?"

"Yeah, while you're in the office, you're connected twenty-four seven. All you have to do is speak into the phone, and it will automatically record your info, license numbers, type of vehicle, any descriptions you can get, be sure to mention how many individuals are in the vehicles. The patrol cars are aware you'll be working there over the night shift so if problems surface, get on 911, and you'll have backup, in about 30 seconds."

"There's a monitor attached just below the office roof line. You can move it left to right a hundred and eighty degrees, and calibrate the lens to adjust focus to your standards. The camera will record license plates, but it might be good to give your observations as well. The more information we have, the better off we'll be."

"How well do you guys know this Ozzie Frick character."

Devitt chuckled. "Frick the prick we call him."

"A typical lowlife, very impressed with himself, and once you know anything about the man, you can't figure out why in the hell he's so impressed. He's been in and out of trouble since he was a kid," Wilkes said.

"We've never seen it here, but word out on the street is he has a tendency to fly off the handle. He's had a few assault charges filed against him over the years, but nothing that ever stuck," Devitt said.

"Like I said, very impressed with himself. Just goes to show you can fool some of the people some of the time," Wilkes added.

We turned onto Daisy's street, and a minute later, we drove past her place. She was sitting on her front porch and gave a close look at the city van as we drove past. There was a nondescript blue car up in the cul-de-sac with two women sitting in the front seat. The rear bumper on the passenger side was smashed and held in place by duct tape, the paint on the car was faded, and the entire hood appeared to be covered in a flat pink primer. As we approached, we could clearly see the women involved in an animated discussion. We drove past them, and Wilkes pulled around in the cul-de-sac then stopped almost next to them. Whatever they were discussing came to a halt. As Wilkes climbed out of the van, the driver's window in the car lowered, and the woman behind the steering wheel called out.

"Is it okay if we park here? It'll only be a couple of minutes, I think."

"Depends on what you're up to," Wilkes said, then opened the rear door in the van and pulled out a toolbox.

The driver's window in the car went back up, and then the vehicle quickly backed down the street and disappeared around the corner.

"Gee, was it something I said?" Wilkes said.

"You better hop into the office," Devitt said to me and gave a nod.

It was blue all right, although the term office was a misnomer. The structure was blue plastic, slightly larger than a phone booth with a curved white plastic roof and a grey plastic ventilation stack sticking out of the roof. The sign on the door said Sanitation Services in red letters. A porta pottie.

"I'm in the shitter?"

They both laughed. "Don't look a gift horse in the mouth. You get to sit around all night long and basically do nothing."

"Yeah, but—"

"That's right. It's a place for butts," Wilkes said, and they both laughed again. "Here, we padlocked it before we left. You wouldn't want to walk in on someone unannounced." He pulled a key out of his pocket and handed it to me. "Enjoy."

"You want a pizza or anything. I'm sure they'd deliver. You can just tell 'em you're right there at the end of the cul-de-sac, it's not like you'd need an address," Devitt said, then chuckled at his own joke.

"No, thanks. So, what time are you showing up in the morning?"

"Right around 8:00. Don't worry, we'll be sure to knock," Wilkes said, then let out another loud laugh.

"I'll see you guys in the morning. Don't be late," I said, then carried my McDonalds bag and my strawberry shake to the so-called office.

"Enjoy your evening," Devitt said, then proceeded to open the toolbox he'd set on the pavement as I made my way into the office. I unlocked the plastic door and stepped inside. There was a 4 x 5 card taped on the back of the toilet seat that read;

Office of the President

Fortunately, the scent was more from industrial cleaner than a number of days in use. I sat down on the seat reserved for the president, the only seat, and did a test run on the recording system.

Fourteen

It was close to six hours before anything really happened. Two cars had driven up the street previously, but they both looked like they'd taken a wrong turn, circled around the cul-de-sac, headed right back down the street and disappeared around the corner. I'd finished my double cheeseburgers and shake a few hours ago when a pair of headlights came up the street and stopped.

From out of nowhere, some guy appeared, casually walked over to the driver's window, chatted for all of fifteen seconds before he was handed something. He headed up toward Ozzie's house and out of my camera's view. I recorded the transaction if you could call it that. A few minutes later, he was back, handed something into the driver's window, and disappeared as the car pulled round, and headed back down the street.

Once the car disappeared, it occurred to me that I hadn't heard anything from Daisy's bullhorn. Traffic gradually began to pick up. At first, a car appeared maybe every ten minutes. Then, shortly after midnight, it was about every couple of minutes, and from about 1:30 in the morning, it was almost nonstop for the next hour or so. The guy taking orders and cash was literally running back and forth to Ozzie's. It slowly dawned on me that it was closing time at the bars and, if you weren't going home, this would be the next logical stop for the clientele.

A good hour later, 2:30ish and the traffic was fading back to a car every fifteen to twenty minutes. At one point, a car pulled up and placed an order while a skinny woman with limp, dark hair hurried out of the passenger side and made a B-line for my office. Fortunately, I'd locked the door from the inside. Not that she didn't try for the better part of a minute to open it. Finally, after swearing a blue streak, she kicked the door. The sound seemed to bounce off the walls for a long moment while she did her business on the far side of the porta pottie. She came back into view as she headed toward the car, zipping her jeans, then turned around, walked back, and kicked the door a final time.

I'd lost track of the number of cars I recorded and the descriptions I'd given. I fell asleep at some point for probably forty-five minutes, and when I woke, the sun was just threatening to rise. For the next two hours, there wasn't any traffic.

Wilkes and Devitt arrived promptly at 7:30. They busied themselves outside for maybe five minutes before Devitt casually strolled over and knocked on the door. "Haskell, you about done in there?" he said and chuckled.

"Barely," I said and opened the door. I had to squint in the sunlight for a moment, then stretched and heard my neck and shoulders sort of snap, crackle, and pop.

"So, how was your night?"

"Surprisingly busy after midnight. Had some woman trying to get in to use the facility."

"Yeah, she probably figured the city put the thing here for her benefit while she waited for her delivery. I tell you, you can't make it up. So, what'd you do?"

"I was a gentleman and let her in."

"You what? Get the hell out of here. Come on, I'll take you home, and you can get some sleep."

Wilkes was working a broom along the curb, and I gave him a nod, then climbed into the van as Devitt got behind the wheel. He lowered the driver's window then said to Wilkes, "I'm going to drop him at home. I'll be back in twenty minutes or so. You need anything?"

Wilkes shook his head and then said, "Get a rundown on activity. Nelson or someone will be viewing the tapes later this morning." He looked past Devitt and said, "You see anything resembling a delivery or the cash pickup vehicle."

I shook my head no, then said, "Nothing, but I think I dozed off for about forty-five minutes. That was a fourteen or fifteen-hour shift. I'm not going to be able to keep that up night after night."

"Yeah, we're going to have to figure something out. Go on home and hit the sack. We can talk later this afternoon."

Devitt raised the window then took off down the street. I didn't see Daisy on the front porch. As we passed her house, Devitt said, "Your girlfriend out there on her bullhorn last night?"

"No, sort of strange, she wasn't, but maybe she had something going on. A lot of activity starting up after 1:00 am. Went on for maybe the next hour and a half. It dawned on me that business more or less dovetails with closing time at the bars."

"Yeah, nice work if you can get it, drink all night then go out and score some drugs, sleep all day, drink all night and then back at it again."

"For maybe forty-five minutes or an hour, that dip-shit that takes orders and grabs the cash was literally running back and forth, trying to keep up with the traffic. I gotta tell you. I was really surprised, nothing short of amazing."

"Depressing is what it is. I'm guessing a lot of these folks don't have two nickels to rub together, but there they are dropping forty or sixty bucks to get high. You'd go nuts if you thought about it for any length of time."

We didn't say much for the rest of the drive to my house. I think I must have dozed off because all of sudden, Devitt was shaking my shoulder. "Hey Haskell, this looks like your dive, so get the hell out of my van and go grab some sleep."

He was right, it was my place. I gave him a nod, told him thanks for the lift, and headed for the front door. Morton was on the couch watching me from the front window. He started barking after I'd taken two steps toward the house. Once I opened the door, he jumped back and forth, and I gave him a heavy rub behind his ears then let him out the back door. I filled his food and water dish, set it on the back porch then climbed upstairs to my bedroom. I took one look at my bed, fell face down onto the pillows, and was sound asleep.

Fifteen

The cellphone vibrating in my front pocket woke me up. It was just a little after two in the afternoon.

"Hello," I said, then cleared my throat and repeated myself. "Hello."

"Haskell, Nelson here. Did I wake you?"

"No, not really," I said and took note of the familiar surroundings in my bedroom and felt a sense of relief that I was actually home.

"How'd you like your office?"

"One of a kind, and with all the amenities," I said.

Nelson laughed at that then said, "Excellent work, by the way. We just finished watching last night's tape. Devitt said you were pretty beat this morning when he dropped you off."

"Yeah. Just for the record, I'm more than happy to help, Lieutenant, but I'm not going to be able to keep up this schedule. That was a fourteen for fifteen-hour shift, and at the end, I was fighting to stay awake. I probably dozed off for about forty-five minutes around four this morning in that so-called office. I get comfortable with those surroundings, and it'll be even longer next time."

"The office works?" he said and laughed.

"I've been in worse places overnight. Yeah, with the exception of some woman wanting to use it after two in the morning, it worked fine. It's a lot better than being crouched down in a hole or lying under some bush. If you watch that tape, there's almost nothing happening other than the occasional buy until after midnight. Business seems to really pick up around closing time for the bars. I told Devitt that sleaze bag hiding in the bushes and taking orders was literally running back and forth for close to an hour, then it died down to barely a crawl after about two-thirty."

"Yeah," Nelson said. "We drew up a chart, and you can gradually see the activity pick up, then like you say, it just drops off around two-thirty. It'll be interesting to see if Friday and Saturday nights run the same."

"Well, I'm game to find out, but I just can't start at four in the afternoon. That has me already pulling eight hours just as the traffic pattern begins to pick up."

"It sounds like you might have a suggestion."

"Actually, I do. What if I park on the far side of the railroad tracks, and walk into the office. It's not like I'm under a street light or anything, so I think I've got a fairly good chance to make it in there unseen in the dark. If Devitt and Wilkes padlocked the office and I had a key, I could get in there, tape the activity for seven or eight hours, and then get out. They could drive me out of there rather than me crossing the tracks in broad daylight, and I'd still be able to record the majority of the traffic, not to mention, stay awake for the entire time." No sound came from the other end of the line. Finally, I said, "You still there?"

"Yeah, just thinking."

"Does it hurt?"

"Don't be a wise ass. Tell you what, let me get in touch with those two. I'll make sure they lock the office then drop the key off here. Maybe plan to be down here around four this afternoon, pick up the key, and we'll give your idea a try. Sound like a plan?"

"I'll see you at four," I said, then disconnected. I placed my cellphone on the far pillow, snuggled under the covers and drifted back to sleep. The phone seemed to ring about a minute later, but as I reached for it, I glanced at the digital clock and realized I'd been asleep for another hour.

"Hello," I groaned.

"You okay? You sound awful."

"Oh, hi, Sophie. How are you?"

"More importantly, how are you? Like I said, you sound awful."

"Oh, sorry. I worked through the night last night, so was just grabbing some sleep."

"Oh, I'm sorry, I didn't mean to wake you. I just—"

"Don't worry about it. It's time to get up anyway. I'll be at it again tonight."

"It doesn't sound very fun."

"The 'f' and the 'u' are correct, but fun isn't the word I'd use to describe it."

"How long are you going to have to do this?"

"I'm not sure, but certainly for a while."

"What about Morton?"

"Morton? Well, he was glad to see me when I got home this morning. He's out in the backyard right now."

"Did he get his morning walk in?"

"You kidding. I had all I could do to make it upstairs and fall into bed. Hopefully, he ran around the backyard while I was asleep. I might be able to take him on a short walk this evening."

"Dev, that's not good for him. He needs to be out at least two times at the very minimum. Four would be better."

"Hey, Sophie, I just worked about a fifteen-hour shift holed up in a small, cramped little area. I get what you're saying and no offense, but four walks with Morton was not the first thing on my list."

"Okay, sorry I brought it up Mr. Crabby, but he has to—"

"Sophie, I don't have the four hours to take him on four separate walks, he'll be okay."

"Well, that explains a lot."

"What did you mean by that?" I said. "Hello, Sophie, you there? Hello."

"Are we through yelling at me?"

"I wasn't yelling," I said, half yelling.

"Oh, boy, and you're doing this again tonight?"

"Midnight to probably seven or eight tomorrow morning. Relax."

"Maybe you should take some of your own advice. Tell you what. Why don't you two come over for a late dinner, say 8:00 tonight? That'll give you time for a short walk, and you won't have to cook or eat at McDonalds or whatever your plan was."

"I wasn't going to eat at McDonalds."

"Yeah, sure. Why don't you both come over and we'll have a late dinner. You can leave Morton here. With this crazy schedule you're working, it's going to put him out of sorts even more than usual."

"That's really kind of you, but you don't have to do this, I'll be fine."

"I'm not worried about you, Dev. See you tonight, and don't forget to bring his bed and a toy he likes. Besides, it will be a good diversion for Lilly, they'll get along famously."

"You don't have to do this, Sophie."

"You're right, I don't, but it would be irresponsible to ignore him while you're out working these hours. How long is this going to last, anyway?"

"I don't know, until we get to the next step, I guess."

"What does that mean?"

"Like I said before, I don't know."

Sixteen

I was in Nelson's office later that afternoon. We were reviewing the tapes and my notes when Devitt and Wilkes showed up. They were dressed in jeans and t-shirts and wearing high visibility vests, just like the day before.

"Anything?" Nelson said, raising his eyebrows as they walked into his office.

"Beyond slow," Wilkes said. "Just the occasional burnout washing up on shore, not even one an hour. No one paid any attention to us. It would appear closing time is when they're doing the majority of their business."

"You see anything of Ozzie Frick?" I asked.

They both shook their heads no, then Devitt said, "All we saw was some guy taking all day to trim the hedge in front that doesn't need trimming. Someone pulls up, he takes their money up to the house."

"Except we never see him go into the house, he heads around the back," Wilkes said.

"Yeah, around to the back, and then he's out front a few minutes later, hands off the buy to the customer, and they drive away."

"We've seen it a million times," Nelson said to me. "This way he's always got a minor amount in his possession or less than a hundred bucks. Anyone nails him, he'll just get a suspended sentence, maybe do a few hours of community service or some other bullshit."

"Be interesting to scope out the back of that place," I said.

"Yeah, except that it's almost a given they'll have a fairly elaborate surveillance setup," Nelson said.

"Not to mention an armed guard or two," Wilkes said.

We all nodded in agreement.

"Oh, before I forget, the key to your office, Haskell," Devitt said. He laughed and tossed a brass key onto a stack of files.

"You're going to walk in tonight," Nelson said. "Maybe park at least a block away, so they don't pick up on your headlights."

"We get the train schedule yet?" Wilkes asked.

"It's random. I'll have copies covering the next two weeks made for you tomorrow morning," Nelson said. He reached over to a stack of files, pulled one out and opened it, then paged through a couple of sheets. "Here it is, only a couple a week. The next one is scheduled to pass by around three-twenty this morning, empty oil cars. After that one, according to this, there isn't another one scheduled until two days from now, supposedly at two-thirty in the morning. Maybe for the record, just note the time it actually passes by tonight, Haskell. Be interesting to see how accurate they are."

I picked up the brass key and placed it in my pocket. "If there's nothing else, I'll see you gentleman here, tomorrow morning."

"Stay safe," Nelson said.

Devitt and Wilkes nodded in agreement.

I headed home and took Morton for a nice long walk. I took a half-hour nap on the living room couch, put Morton's bed in the car, let Morton hop into the backseat, and headed out to Sophie's. We stopped and picked up flowers and a bottle of wine on the way. I pulled in front of Sophie's at eight on the dot. A blue BMW with a red convertible top was parked at the end of her driveway. As I got out of the car, Sophie opened the front door and waved, a woman stepped out from behind her and headed for the BMW. She was an attractive redhead with a blonde streak in her hair.

"You must be the guy I've heard so much about, Dev is it?" she said and held out her hand.

"Yeah, Dev Haskell," I said, taking her hand.

"I'm Sophie's friend, B.B. We live just up the street, nice to finally meet you. Enjoy," she said, then hopped behind the wheel of the BMW and backed out of the driveway.

I watched her back into the street then waved as she drove off. At that moment, a white paneled van came around the bend. It was one of those retro Chevy things with the extended hood with a big Chevy logo on the front. It looked like something out of the 40's, and as it passed, it gave us a little honk, then drove around the next bend and disappeared from sight.

Morton barked from inside my car, and I let him out then grabbed the flowers, the wine, Morton's bed, and two of his favorite chew toys.

"Oh, look at you, all that stuff, you didn't have to do this, Dev," Sophie said, as I handed her the flowers.

"It could be worse. I could be making deliveries in that white van at eight at night."

"Yeah, always heading up to the Dwyer house. I swear they must be ordering things online every day, seven days a week."

"Dwyer? Would that be Dennis Dwyer, the attorney?"

"Yeah, as a matter of fact, it is. Do you know him?"

"Not really, just heard his name mentioned a few times. Seems to do pretty well for himself," I said, recalling Nelson's comment the other day about Ozzie Frick's place being a Dennis Dwyer operation. But then, how did that get Tubby Gustafson involved? It still didn't make sense.

"Here, we picked up a bottle of wine for you, too," I said, handing Sophie the bottle.

"Oh, Dev, really, so unnecessary. We're glad to watch Morton for a while, it's really not a problem. I told Lilly he'll be staying here for a bit, and she's all excited."

I looked at Sophie but didn't say anything.

"Come on, Morton, let's go say hi to Lilly," Sophie said. Morton's tail started wagging, and he thrust his nose in-between Sophie's thighs. She was wearing short shorts and she sort of squirmed. "Oh-oh-oh, Morton, you have a very cold nose."

"Oh, yeah, sorry about that, probably because he likes to put his head out the window when we're driving down the interstate."

"Of course he does," Sophie said, and gave Morton a rub behind his ears. "Okay, come on inside, boys," she said and held the front door open for us.

I stepped inside and was about to drop Morton's bed next to the door, when Sophie said, "Oh, no, Dev. Bring that into the kitchen, that's where Lilly sleeps."

"You sure, I mean, well, Morton and a female dog. He can't seem to help himself, and he sometimes isn't on his best behavior."

"Well, gee. Now I wonder who he learned that from?"

"Hey, come on, I've never tried to ride you outside of a coffee shop."

"He did that? Oh, funny. Come to think of it, I guess that's true, you haven't, but only because we haven't been to a coffee shop, yet. No, now, I'm serious, bring that bed into the kitchen."

"Okay, but don't say I didn't warn you."

"Maybe just a little more positive attitude, Mister," she said, then she sort of wrinkled her nose as I walked past her. “Say, when was the last time you washed that bed?”

“You can wash these?”

“Put it in the kitchen, by the back door, next to Lilly’s bed. It’ll be a good way to get him accustomed to interacting with others. He has to learn this behavior sooner or later, so we might as well get started.”

Seventeen

We ate a nice chicken dinner at the kitchen counter. Sophie seemed more interested in Morton and Lilly than me, and I left Sophie's around 11:30 frustrated that my not so subtle hints went unaddressed.

A little before midnight, I pulled to a stop in front of a nice-looking house probably built in the mid-fifties. The house was a single-story affair painted dark green with white trim, in a style referred to as a rambler. What looked to have originally been an attached garage, had at some point been turned into another bedroom. A car was parked in the driveway that led up to what was now a bedroom window.

I had parked a good block away and across the railroad tracks from the porta pottie office. I got out of the car and glanced up and down the block. At this hour, most of the homes looked to be shut down for the night.

I walked up the block toward the railroad tracks. One home had the living room curtains pulled back, and I could see a kid who looked like he was maybe sixteen stretched out on a couch watching television. All the lights were off, and the room was bathed in blue light from the television that occasionally flickered. Upon a closer look, the kid appeared to be sound asleep.

I waited on the far side of the railroad tracks for maybe ten minutes until a car headed up the street and pulled to a stop in front of Ozzie's house. The same guy as the night before suddenly appeared from nowhere and hurried over to the driver's side window chatted for a few seconds then hurried back toward Ozzie's house. I waited a long moment before I hurried across the tracks, cautiously unlocked the padlocked door, and stepped inside the porta pottie.

Everything appeared to be okay, and I quickly adjusted the camera lens and focused first on the license plate and then the occupants. A moment later, the delivery man was back with their purchase, and they drove off not more than five seconds later.

I attempted to focus on the delivery man, but he disappeared out of camera range before I could zoom in on him. I made a mental note that getting his image would be one of tonight's goals. Much like the previous night, business slowly began to pick up over the next hour then started into full swing right around one-thirty. By two in the morning, the deliveryman was running back and forth. More than once, the cars were two and three deep waiting to place their orders. A little after three, traffic had slowed back down to a customer every fifteen or twenty minutes. I settled back and opened up the lunch Sophie had packed for me. A roast beef sandwich on homemade sourdough bread, a bag of Bar-B-Que potato chips, an apple, and two chocolate chip cookies.

At exactly three-thirty a train rolled past. I cracked the door about an inch and watched maybe ten minutes' worth of oil cars heading north. Given the direction they were traveling, I figured they were probably headed out to the Bakken Oil Field up in North Dakota.

Car traffic had slowed to just two or three an hour, then stopped altogether. Just before four in the morning, a white paneled van drove up the street, turned, and headed up the driveway without stopping. It was a retro 40's looking thing, with a long, rounded hood and a Chevy logo on the front of the hood. It moved fast enough going up the drive that I wasn't able to focus on the license plate. Fifteen minutes later, I got a good shot of the license plate as it headed out of the driveway and back down the street.

At seven forty-five the next morning, Devitt and Wilkes pulled up and unloaded some sort of equipment out of the back of the truck they were driving then stood around leisurely sipping cups of coffee from a thermos. Once they'd finished their coffee, Devitt took a look around, then casually strolled over and knocked on the door.

"Time to wake up, Sleeping Beauty."

I unlocked the door and stepped outside. Once again, the daylight was blinding for the first few seconds.

"You guys enjoy your coffee?"

"Just trying to bore anyone who might be interested in watching us," Devitt said. "How were things last night?"

"Pretty much a repeat of the previous night. Gradually building until about one-thirty when it got absolutely crazy for maybe an hour then quickly tapered off. One thing I did catch, a white paneled van pulled up the driveway and behind the house just before five this morning, a Chevy retro 40's sort of thing. It was up there behind the house for maybe fifteen minutes before it headed back out. Got a good shot of the license plate on the way out."

"You think it might have been a product delivery or maybe a cash pick up?" Devitt said.

"I think there's a good possibility it was both. We'll see if he shows up again tomorrow morning."

"Be interesting to see where he goes from here. Anyone pound on the door to use the facilities last night?"

"No, thank God. I don't need that kind of attention. Hey, you want the key so you can lock this thing up at the end of the day?"

"Thanks, but not necessary. You hang onto the key. I'll just close the padlock when we leave, keep any freeloaders from using it, you can unlock it whenever you get here."

"Okay, then I'm taking off. Hope you have a nice quiet day."

"Thanks, Haskell. Hey, in case we didn't say anything, thanks for doing this. We'll get this Ozzie Frick prick sooner rather than later, and that'll be due in no small part to you volunteering to help. It's much appreciated."

"My pleasure, and same to you guys for taking the day shift. Now, if you'll excuse me, I have an appointment with a long hot shower and a bed. Stay safe."

"Same to you. See you tomorrow morning."

I climbed into the van, and Wilkes drove me over to my car.

Eighteen

I headed home, parked in the driveway, tossed two burritos in the microwave then phoned Sophie. After four rings, I got dumped into her voice mail.

"Hi Sophie, it's Dev. Just wanted to let you know I'm finished for the night and home safe and sound. I'm going to grab a shower and hit the sack, so I'll try and call back this afternoon." I thought for a second or two then said, "Hey, I'm going to put my phone on airplane mode, so don't bother to call me back. I'll give you a call later on. Thanks for taking care of Morton, hope he wasn't too big of a pain. Catch you later," I said and hung up. I quickly put my phone on airplane mode, took the burritos out of the microwave, wolfed them down, and went upstairs to bed.

I think it was a woman named Jessica who left one of those eye masks for sleeping like the airlines pass out on long flights. Except she had been into some kinky sort of stuff, and the thing was edged in fuzzy pink feathers and featured a pair of eyes painted in blue glitter. Anyway, I put it on and slept until a little after four. Once awake, it took a minute or two before I sat up in bed then phoned Sophie.

"God, are you even alive?" she answered.

"Oh, hey, how's it going?"

"I was worried about you, got your message this morning, I must have just missed your call."

"Yeah, talk about a long night. I was really beat. In fact, I just woke up. I'm not even out of bed. You're the first person I called."

"Oh, that's sweet."

"So, what's Morton been into?"

"Into? Nothing, to tell you the truth, he's been really good. He and Lilly are outside in the back playing with a soccer ball."

"He's playing with a soccer ball?"

"Well, it's not really a soccer ball, it's more like an exercise ball. I've got four of them out there, and Lilly moves them back and forth, sort of like sheep herding only without the sheep. She's showing him how to chase it around, pushing it with her nose."

"And he's actually doing it?"

"Well, actually, no. I mean he was, sort of. Right now, he's laying down and watching her push the ball back and forth."

"Yeah, that sounds more like him. But he's not causing any problems?"

"No, not really."

"Not really?"

"No, he's not. He's being very good."

I wondered how much good behavior Morton had left in him. It couldn't be much.

"So, he's okay for another night?"

"Oh, Dev, we're counting on the entire week, don't worry about it."

"Are you sure? I mean it's nice, no wait, it's really great of you to offer, but I know how he gets. I mean, you're taking on a lot here."

"I always enjoy a challenge."

"Yeah, well, he can certainly be that, and a lot more. Okay, well, I'm going to check in with my better half down at the police station. Any problems give me a ring. I'm not kidding, Sophie, call if he becomes a pain."

"Thank you, but we'll be just fine. You take care of yourself, and I'll talk to you tomorrow," she said, then hung up.

So far, so good. I called Lieutenant Nelson next. "Nelson," he answered.

"Hey, Lieutenant, Dev Haskell."

"Haskell, great job on last night's recordings. You'll be back at it tonight?"

"Yeah, planning on being back there right around midnight. I'll be there until Wilkes and Devitt arrive tomorrow morning. You get anything on the license number of that van around five this morning?"

"That white van? Not that I'm aware of. I haven't personally watched the tape. Just reviewed your comments, but if you had it recorded, I should have the results by the end of the day or first thing in the morning. Anything out of the ordinary last night?"

"No, other than that van showing up, and it might be unique only because I fell asleep at about the same time the day before. Otherwise, the traffic pattern was essentially the same as the previous night, slow then building until it's jammed for maybe ninety minutes around closing time. More than a few times, cars were lined up waiting to make a buy. The guy exchanging cash and product was literally running back and forth."

"Jesus Christ. Okay, well, you're on for more of the same tonight?"

"Yeah, same routine as last night. Wilkes and Devitt lock the office when they leave, and I'm in there right around midnight. I'll be there until they show up around eight the following morning."

"Can't thank you enough, Haskell. Say, anything from your girlfriend down the block?"

"Daisy? No, funny you should ask, nothing the last two nights."

"You say anything to her?" Nelson asked.

"No. I saw her that first night when I drove in with the guys. She was sitting on her front porch, but I haven't seen her since, and I certainly haven't heard anything from her."

"Hmm-mmm, a bit strange that," Nelson said.

"You worried?"

"Not yet. I'll let you know if I am. You stay safe and enjoy yourself."

"Thanks, I will."

Nineteen

I drove out to Sophie's in Burnsville. I phoned her when I was about ten minutes away.

"Hi, Dev," she answered.

"Hi, Sophie. Hey, would it be all right if I swung by for a few minutes? I just wanted to say goodnight to Morton."

"Oh, that would be just fine. How nice of you to think of him. He's doing just fine, had a really good day. They're both lying in bed just now, exhausted after all that running around earlier."

"Great, I'll see you in about twenty minutes."

I drove past Sophie's about eight minutes later, the dark blue BMW with the red top was parked at the end of the driveway again. I drove past and continued around the bend. The homes grew decidedly larger and more elegant on the lake side of the road. About three minutes past Sophie's, was a massive two-story red brick place. It had a circular drive leading up to the front door and a brick wall topped with wrought iron surrounding the property. Double wrought iron gates barred any entry into the circular drive.

The front of the place featured luscious trimmed bushes against the house and at least three security cameras, not counting the one at the wrought iron gates. I slowed as I drove past and saw three nice looking cars parked in the circular drive, a large, black SUV, a shiny, four-door Mercedes either black or dark blue, and some other red sporty thing I couldn't identify that looked way out of my price range. I didn't see a white paneled van anywhere.

The name above the brass mailbox attached to the brick wall read D. Dwyer and below that the address, 666 Lake Shore Drive. I continued along the road for maybe another half mile, then pulled a U-turn, went past Dwyer's place again, and then drove back to Sophie's. The BMW was just backing out of the driveway, as I approached Sophie's. Redheaded B.B. was behind the wheel. She honked and waved out the window at me then continued up the street.

Sophie was standing in the doorway. "Dev," she said, opening the front door. "Thanks for stopping by, you didn't have to, but it's great to see you. Come on in." She held the door open for me then stepped aside as I entered, we exchanged a quick kiss.

Lily was suddenly there, watching. "Oh, Lilly, look who's here, Morton's dad," Sophie said. Lilly gave me a sniff, then turned and headed back into the kitchen area. I followed Sophie. The wall-mounted television was playing in the kitchen, some guy harping on about the latest thing congress had failed to accomplish.

"Can I get you a glass of wine or a beer?"

"Oh, gee, thanks Sophie, not that I wouldn't love one, but I'm on the job again tonight, and I'd be asleep halfway through it if I have something to drink. But, don't let me hold you up, help yourself."

"Actually, I've already got a glass going. B.B. and I were gossiping."

"Yeah, I saw her on her way out, she seems very nice."

"She's my best friend, no secrets between the two of us." She picked up the remote from the kitchen counter. "Let me just turn this off, don't even know why I watch the news, it just gets more and more depressing every day. You sure I can't get you something?"

"Thanks, but yeah, I'm positive." I looked over at Morton. His bed was in the corner near the door leading out to the patio. He raised his head as I came into view, but he didn't get out of his bed. I walked over to him, gave him a good rub behind his ears, and his tail began to thump against the floor.

"I think Lilly really wore him out. They were chasing one another around then playing with the exercise balls. He was just about ready to drift off to sleep when you rang the doorbell."

"But he's been behaving?"

"Not a problem, he's been great."

"Really? Sorry, didn't mean to sound so surprised. It's just that I'm not used to a lot of positive feedback. I mean, usually he's gotten into something by this point and—"

"Will you just relax. I told you he's fine, besides Lilly can be a little bit high energy and he's probably just plain old worn out. That's not all bad."

"I'll say. Well, again, Sophie, I really appreciate it, thanks so much for everything."

"God, you're making it sound like he's been here for a month, it's barely been twenty-four hours. Relax, they're doing just fine. How are things in the world of crime going?"

"Boring, which I guess is a good thing. I sure don't need any trouble. We're just gathering information at this point, what the police do with that is up to them. You're helping with Morton makes it a lot easier for me."

"I've told you it's so not a problem. Hey, are you up for some frozen yogurt and maybe some homemade caramel sauce topping?"

"Mmm-mmm."

"I'll take that as a yes. It's so nice of you to stop by," she said, then pulled the yogurt container out of the freezer and a large mason jar from the refrigerator. She placed a couple of scoops of frozen yogurt into two bowls. It looked like there were pieces of chocolate embedded in the frozen yogurt, then she poured a rich looking caramel sauce from the mason jar. One bowl held decidedly more than the other, and she passed it over to me.

"You sure you don't want this one?"

"Actually, I'd love it, but it would take me two weeks to wear it off. It's so not fair, guys just have to think about losing weight, and you automatically do. I starve myself, work out for a week straight, and put on eight ounces."

"Must have something to do with my clear conscience," I said and took another spoonful of the caramel sauce.

"Or the lack of any conscience."

The caramel sauce was delicious and despite having about twice the amount in my bowl, I finished before Sophie was barely halfway through her serving.

"Would you like some more?" she said, meaning anything but.

"It was delicious, but that was my limit, really good."

"Glad you enjoyed it. What time do you have to be there tonight?"

"Right around midnight, it's just me, so no one is really watching the clock."

"Gee, and it's not even ten. I wonder what we could do for the next two hours?"

Twenty

I pulled up in front of the rambler at half-past twelve. I stepped out of the car, tucked in my t-shirt, buckled my belt, and hurried down the street toward the railroad tracks. All the lights were off in the houses, including the one where the kid had been asleep on the couch last night. I kept thinking about Sophie as I hurried along and caught just the slightest scent of her perfume. I stopped at the railroad tracks and waited for a car to show up in front of Ozzie Frick's.

I only had to wait for a minute or two before a pair of headlights made their way up the street, turned around in the cul-de-sac, then stopped. The same guy, as on previous nights, suddenly appeared, took their order, and hurried away. Once he disappeared, I quickly made my way across the railroad tracks, unlocked the porta pottie and stepped inside. I was able to get the camera up and focused, recording the license plate on the car before he was back with the delivery. I made a point of recording his image as he disappeared behind the hedge.

The night was pretty much the same as the preceding ones, a little bit busier perhaps, but then again, we were that much closer to the weekend. At one point, two women left their car and made their way over to the porta pottie, obviously on a mission to use the facilities. They were even less happy with their results than the skinny blonde woman the other night.

"Are you f'ing kidding me, come on, hurry up in there," one of them shouted then kicked the door three or four times.

A few seconds later, the other woman shouted, "Hurry up in there, will you, we really need to go. Hey," she screamed and pounded on the door. "Is anyone even in there?"

I didn't respond.

One of them tugged at the door hard enough that I thought she might break the lock off. I grabbed onto the door handle and held it closed, hoping she wouldn't rip the thing off its hinges.

A male voice suddenly called out from the car, "Janice, come on, let's go."

"Some bastard's in there and won't unlock the door."

"Get your ass over here now, or we're leaving you. Come on, now."

"Would you just wait a minute, we really have to go."

I heard the car accelerate for a brief moment, and one of the women yelled, "Okay, okay, God, would you calm down? We're coming, we're coming."

One of them gave the door a final kick then screamed, "Your guy is leaving with us, you slut, and we're gonna screw his brains out." She kicked the door again and then ran back to the car, and they drove off.

So much for manners, but then again maybe I was looking in the wrong place. Those two chicks and Sophie were absolute worlds apart.

The rest of the night was relatively uneventful, other than being a lot busier. Traffic died down noticeably for the last three hours compared to earlier nights, but that might have been due to the rain. It wasn't a heavy rain, but rather a steady drizzle, the kind that made you have to set the wipers on the car about every five seconds.

The white paneled van headed up the drive at a little after five. This time, I was able to get images of it coming and going. Once I recorded the license plate, I focused on the driver, although I wasn't too sure how those images were going to turn out. It was raining lightly, so there was a good chance the image wouldn't be very good. Just like before, after about fifteen minutes, it drove back down the drive, out onto the street, and disappeared around the corner.

A little after eight, Wilkes and Devitt arrived. They were dressed in yellow rain pants and jackets. The jackets had a hood on them that was pulled up over their baseball caps. They had the high visibility green vests on over their rain jackets. They unloaded shovels and brooms from the back of the truck, then sat in the cab drinking coffee and eating donuts for the next half hour before Devitt finally knocked on the door of the office.

"You nice and dry in there?" he asked, as I opened the door.

"Yeah, but there's no coffee or donuts, thanks for saving me some."

"But we didn't," he said, with a questioning look on his face.

"Yeah, I know. Nothing out of the ordinary last night except there was more activity. Things pretty much shut down, once the rain started up."

"Yeah, well, we wouldn't want the burnouts ruining their hair in the rain, now, would we?" Devitt said.

"Lock is resting on the toilet seat, enjoy the weather," I said.

"Behave," Devitt said then held the door for me. I gave a slight wave to Wilkes as he slipped back into the truck cab then hurried across the tracks back to my car. On the way home, I stopped at a McDonalds drive-through and got three Egg McMuffins and promptly ate all three before I got home. I put my phone back on airplane mode, then stepped into a hot shower where I remained for a good fifteen minutes. I crawled into bed, donned the eye mask edged in fuzzy pink feathers with the glittery blue eyes that Jessica left behind and promptly fell asleep.

Twenty-one

I woke a little after three, sat up in bed then took my phone off airplane mode. I'd missed three calls and had one message waiting for me. The message was from Sophie. The other two calls were from Lieutenant Nelson. He hadn't bothered to leave a message, so I phoned him first.

"Nelson," he half-shouted into the phone, giving the impression he was really busy after just one word.

"Hi, Lieutenant, Dev Haskell. You phoned a couple of times. Sorry, I missed the calls, but I was asleep."

"Well, God only knows you certainly need your beauty sleep. You must have been awfully tired if you slept through both of my calls," he said, not sounding too happy that I was tired after working midnight to eight for free.

I took that to mean someone actually reporting to him and on the payroll had better answer his phone calls, but then again, I wasn't on any payroll, I was a volunteer. A volunteer they needed. None the less, I thought it prudent not to mention the fact I'd placed my phone on airplane mode. "Everything okay?"

"Yeah, reviewing your summary of the night's activity, it looks like you were pretty busy last night."

"Yeah, I was, and I expect tonight to be even busier, if only because it's one day closer to the weekend."

"I see that van was there again, just about the same time as yesterday, and it's there for no more than fifteen minutes."

"I don't know if you had a chance to view the tape, but—"

"Actually, I didn't," Nelson said.

"I recorded the license plate then focused on the driver. Not sure how clear the image will appear since it was raining at the time, but I was hoping you or someone there might actually be able to recognize the driver."

"I'll give it a look. We'll pass the image around here to see if it rings a bell with anyone. You up for another shift tonight?" he asked.

"I wouldn't dream of missing it."

"Wonderful. Anything else I can do for you?"

"No, Lieutenant. I'll be on the same routine tonight. I get there about midnight and then hang around until Wilkes and Devitt show up in the morning. Are they picking up any unique activity?"

"No. Like you, they seem to be dealing with a similar pattern. Increasing activity as we draw closer to the weekend. They note a bit of a bump in business over the noon hour, and we surmise that may be the same around dinner time as the normal workday ends. But it's nothing compared to the traffic you're catching from midnight until after closing time. I guess all that comes as no real surprise. With a half dozen drinks under their belts, the odds of people making some sort of stupid decision increase exponentially."

"Go back to that van for a moment," I said. "Did you ever get a hit on that license plate?"

"I'm pretty sure we did, I think I've got the results here, somewhere. Can you hang on for a moment, and I'll check?" He set the phone down, and I could hear what sounded like him rifling through a stack of papers. Suddenly, he was back on the line. "Yeah, here it is, the vehicle is a white, 2007 Chevy HHR panel van. It's one of those vehicles designed in a 40's retro style."

"Yeah, that sounds like it, there's a big Chevy logo on the front of the hood. Actually, the thing looks kind of cool. I'm a little surprised they didn't go for something less noticeable. Who is it registered to."

"It's a commercial registration, a company called Abco."

"Abco? Never heard of them."

"You're not alone. They'd be a mystery to most people. Their business address is a PO Box. The actual business location, according to our most recent records, is down on West Seventh Street. Far as I know, they're still up on the third floor of that building."

"What do they do?" I said.

"Apparently, their business is business."

"What?"

"Some time back, one of our team members posed as someone selling yellow pages ads."

"People still buy those?"

"Not that I'm aware of, which makes it the perfect cover to check out an address. She was just trying to get into the place. This would have been a few months back, maybe even a year ago. If I recall, the place was just a small room with a phone, a desk, and four guys supposedly *working*," he said, emphasizing the word to suggest anything but working.

"Get this," Nelson half laughed. "The report said there were cards and poker chips scattered across the desk. Business can't be that good if all of them have to share the same phone. I think she said there was a laptop on the desk tuned into some radio station or maybe a cartoon. I can't recall which. Bogus setup, either way."

"That doesn't make any sense."

"Gee, really? You think? You at all curious who might own this so-called business that doesn't make any sense?"

"Yeah. Who?"

"Another organization, just as fake. That one is called Molly Malone, LLC."

"Is that supposed to mean something to me? I've never heard of it, although the name rings a bell."

"Haskell, Molly Malone, get it? 'She wheels her wheelbarrow, through the streets broad and narrow,'" Nelson sung the line to me. "The tart with the cart. Get it? Hello? It's a joke. And of course, you never heard of these companies before because they're both shell companies. So, how about I just cut to the chase, and I give you the owners real name. You ready?"

"Who is he?"

"The name Molly Dwyer ring any bells?"

"She related to Dennis Dwyer?"

"Ding-dong. She's his wife."

"And this place is down on West Seventh Street? You got an address on the building?"

"Yeah 1035, and no, I don't want you going down there. In fact, I don't want you anywhere near the place."

"That's gotta be just a couple blocks from my office."

"Oh, great, stupid me. Listen, do me a favor and just forget I even gave you that address. In fact, I don't even want you to drive by the building."

"Why, you got it under surveillance?"

"If only. You kidding? We got you giving us volunteer hours, and I'm pulling out what little hair I have left after a three-hour budget meeting this morning and another one scheduled for tomorrow morning. With all that going on, you think we got the funds to watch a building where nothing happens? It's just some idiots sitting around telling stupid jokes and playing cards. Nothing's happening there, but if the state or the county ever checked the place out, there'd be people there, it's occupied, they got a phone line, pay rent, and they'll be happy to tell you that their business is business."

"The state or county really stops by and checks them out?"

"God, no. I'm sure these Abco idiots pay whatever fees they have to, don't cause a problem, and, as long as the check is good, no one at County or State level complains. Nice work if you can get it."

Twenty-two

The message Sophie left was short and to the point. Just two words. "Call me," she said, not sounding at all pleased. I called her back, and she finally answered on the fourth or fifth ring, which gave me a brief moment to try and figure out what it was I'd screwed up or forgotten.

"Dev?" she said, sounding like one of my pissed off grade school teachers.

"Hi, Sophie, what's wrong?"

"Why do you think somethings wrong?" she said, sounded even less happy than a moment before.

"I thought I might have picked it up in your voice." I was still trying to recall what it was I'd done wrong when it suddenly came to me in a flash. "Morton. What did he do now?"

"Why do you think Morton's done anything?"

"What's he done, Sophie? Believe me. No one knows better than me what he can be like."

"Well, he's in the process of taking a time out right now. Both he and Lilly are reflecting."

Reflecting? Morton was probably taking a nap. "Did he break something? Did he leave a puddle on your carpet? Did he chew—?"

"No, actually, nothing like that, no real damage. But, if you really want to know, he ate my breakfast, the entire breakfast."

"He ate—"

"My breakfast. All of it. I had a plate with an omelette of two egg whites, a piece of gluten-free bread, and a strip of low-fat turkey bacon sitting on the counter. I was gone for no more than sixty seconds, and when I came back into the kitchen, my plate had been licked clean."

I was thinking the way she described the breakfast she should be thankful Morton saved her the trouble of having to eat it. Not that Morton had ever really been known to be picky when it came to someone else's food. "Oh, Sophie, I'm sorry. Would you like me to come and get him?"

"No. What I want is for you to stay away, today, all day and then every day after that unless you hear differently from me."

"Hey, I didn't steal your breakfast, so don't go after me. But if he's doing that sort of misbehavior, he's apparently adapted to his new surroundings and feels quite comfortable. Let me come and get him before it's something a lot worse than low-fat turkey bacon and gluten-free bread."

"Oh, that's not the worst of it."

“Did he break a china plate?” I was thinking one of the plates with the Chocolate Labrador in the center. Yea, Morton, one down and only seven plates to go.

“No, hardly.”

Damn.

“But he did manage to pass at least some of it on to Lilly. She’s on a very strict diet, Dev. I came back into the kitchen, and she had egg white all over her mouth. Apparently, he didn’t bother to share the turkey bacon with her.”

Lucky Lilly. “Turkey bacon?”

“That’s not the point, besides you’re not to come out here. We’re in the process of determining exactly who is in the alpha position, so Morton is currently taking a time out in the pantry for the next thirty minutes, and Lilly is confined to her bed. Besides, I’ve got a call in to the vet, and I’m just waiting for a response on how that food will affect her system. I just may have to bring her in and have her stomach pumped, the poor little thing.”

“You sure I can’t come out and just take him off your hands. It wouldn’t be a problem and might just save you a lot of headaches down the road.”

“No offense, Dev, but that is exactly what he’d like right now. I mean this in the nicest way to say it, but it’s like he’s been living in a fraternity house or something. He needs some discipline, in fact, if you don’t mind my saying, he really needs a lot of discipline.”

“It sounds like mission impossible to me.”

“Which is exactly why he’s the way he is.”

"You're sure?"

"I'm positive. Now, not another word. He has another eleven minutes in the pantry, then I plan on discussing his behavior with him, and he'll spend the rest of the afternoon out in the backyard. Lilly will remain in the house, her yard privileges have been revoked for the afternoon."

"You run a tight ship, Sophie."

"Consistency is the key, Dev. Believe me, Morton will ultimately be the better for it. You just wait till you see how well he'll be doing by the end of the week."

"Yeah, if he hasn't driven you nuts before then."

"Like I said, we'll get along just fine once he realizes who is in charge."

"Okay, but call me if it gets to be too much."

"We'll be fine, thank you for your concern," she said and hung up.

I think I was beginning to feel sorrier for Morton.

Twenty-three

It was just a little after five, and I figured it wouldn't be a bad idea to check in at my real office and see how Louie was doing. Given the hour, he was probably already across the street at The Spot bar.

Louie Laufen was my office mate. An attorney who had somehow managed to dodge any and all attempts at disbarment. On any given day of the week, he wore one of five different, wrinkled suits. He used a picnic table for his desk, and he spent more time at The Spot bar than he did in the office. I loved him.

On the way down to The Spot, I just happened to drive past 1035 West Seventh. It turned out to be a three-story red brick building with a cornerstone listing 1885 as the date of construction. There was a driveway on the east side of the building that led to a parking area. I pulled in and drove along the building to the parking area in the rear.

The parking lot had a cyclone fence around it with a row of concertina wire on top of the fence. It was laid out for a dozen parking places, all but two were empty. A black SUV, with dark tinted windows, was backed into a spot against the fence so that it faced the rear of the building. Parked up against the building with it's white, 40's retro style nose almost touching the brick wall was an HHR 2007 white Chevy paneled van, just like the one I'd recorded coming in and out of Ozzie Frick's place on the last two nights. I figured the odds of there being two vehicles like that in the seven-county metro area would be something like about one percent. I wrote down the license number on the van and pulled into one of the parking places. Then I backed up alongside the white paneled van so I could drive out of the parking lot.

At exactly the same time, the rear door to the building suddenly opened up, and three rather large individuals walked out. They were in the midst of laughing when they stopped and stared at me, just getting ready to pull out. The smiles immediately left their faces, and they spread out across the parking lot, basically blocking any forward progress I was about to make, well unless I wanted to run one of them down.

The guy closest to me twirled his right hand, signaling me to roll down my window. He was a muscular guy, big, but not fat. His arms hung out from his sides as if he was carrying a box under either arm, all due to incredibly large bicep and pectoral muscles. He had broad shoulders, a thick neck, and he wore a grey strappy t-shirt, the kind often referred to as a wife-beater. The words *'No Pain, No Gain'* were printed across the front of the t-shirt in bold black letters. I could see the six-pack his abs formed beneath the t-shirt, as he took a step toward me.

I rolled down the window, smiled very politely, and gave him my best attempt at groveling, "Good afternoon, sir."

"What the hell do you think you're doing back here?"

"I missed my turn. I'm meeting someone up at The Spot bar. I was watching two women cross the street, not paying attention to where I was going and missed the turn. So I cut through here, thinking it would bring me back to Randolph Avenue. I didn't know the lot was fenced off."

"The Spot, who you meeting there?"

"My lawyer."

"A Lawyer. You in some kind of trouble?"

"Ummm, more like a bit of bad luck, cops nailed me on a DUI," I lied. "Not my first, unfortunately. I'm just hoping he can get me off, maybe have it pled down to some lesser charge. Never fails, they're out there going after some poor guy like me when there's real criminals running around."

He nodded like this made perfect sense then said, "This here is private like, probably best for you we don't see your sorry ass back here, ever again."

"I got no problem with that, sir."

"Okay, better get the hell out of here and, ahh, good luck. You're gonna need it, meeting with a lawyer."

"He's okay. Right now, I just need these charges to go away."

He nodded again, suggesting maybe he'd been in a similar position a time or two. "It's okay, let him go," he said to the other muscle-bound guys then waved them over to the side. They both gave me a look, appearing quite a bit less friendly than the guy I just talked to.

I gave a little wave, yelled, "Thank you," then drove out of the lot. I had to wait at the corner for the light to change. I had my blinker on signaling a lefthand turn. First, the SUV drove out of the lot, then the white paneled van followed right behind it. They pulled up behind me, and I was worried the doors might suddenly open on the SUV. If they did, I was going to run the red light, but they suddenly put their left blinkers on, and I figured all was well.

Once the light changed, I waited for a half dozen cars to pass then turned left onto Randolph Ave. The Spot bar was up about four blocks. Luckily for me, there was a parking place almost in front, and I quickly pulled in. A moment later, the SUV drove past, and gave a little honk on the horn. The thug driving the white paneled van was right behind the SUV. He slowed down and gave me a long look as he drove past. I felt like giving him the finger, but common sense prevailed, and I didn't. Then, I watched as they headed up the hill to the Interstate 35E entrance. I presumed they would follow that out to Burnsville, drive past Sophie's house, and ultimately into Dennis Dwyer's circular drive.

Twenty-four

Louie was on his usual stool, just inside the front door at The Spot. "Just in time," he said, the moment he saw it was me coming in the door. "Mike, I better have another, Dev's buying."

Mike looked at me, and I nodded. "Just a Coke for me, I'm pulling a night shift," I said.

"Oh, come on, one won't hurt," Louie said just a little too loudly, and I immediately got the feeling he might have already been here for a while.

"You're right, Louie, one won't hurt. Problem with me is, I won't stop at one, so it's just better if I don't start."

Mike slid Louie's refilled whiskey glass across the bar and then popped the top on a can of Coke for me and set it on the bar.

"Thanks, pal," Louie said and took a drink.

I sipped the Coke for a moment then said, "Let me ask you something, Louie. What do you know about shell companies?"

"Shell companies? You mean a company existing as a legal entity that has no significant assets, independent business operations, or anything else and is often owned by some other company and God forbid, possibly used on some occasions for illegal purposes?"

"Yeah, I suppose," I said, trying to get my head around what Louie had just rattled off.

"I don't know anything about them," he said and took another drink. "So, why do you ask?"

Fortunately, Mike had moved down to the far end of the bar to serve three guys who looked like they'd just finished running a marathon. All three of them were wearing running shoes, shorts, and sweat-soaked shirts. Two of them were wearing sweaty baseball caps.

I focused back on Louie. "Why do I ask? I'm working on something, and I think this shell company, if I can call it that, has a vehicle licensed to it and it's running drugs to a distribution point, then picking up cash receipts and bringing them back."

"You know this for a fact?"

"I'm pretty sure the vehicle that's registered to the company is doing that. I haven't seen the drugs in the car. I haven't seen the cash I suspect they're hauling, either. I have seen them at a house that is dealing drugs. The car, it's actually a paneled van, pulls into the place around four in the morning, leaves about fifteen minutes later. It's done that for the last three days. I expect it to do it again tonight, or well, actually tomorrow morning around four."

"Sounds plausible, although a shell company isn't exactly an entry-level operation. So, my first sense would be that wherever you've seen this vehicle, that's one of a number of pickups and deliveries that it's making."

I thought about that for a moment. It seemed to make sense. "Let me ask you something else, you know of a guy named Dennis Dwyer?"

"Sean's kid?" Louie said, then sat back and seemed to study me for a long moment.

"If you say so."

"I sort of know him, not the nicest guy I can think of, the term asshole immediately springs to mind. He's maybe a little older than you, married, and I believe last time I checked, his wife was a redhead."

"I think her name is Molly," I said.

"Yeah, that's the guy. Let me give you some free advice. If he wants to hire you, it would be best to stay away. Nothing good will come of it, no matter what he offers to pay you. If you've already taken him on as a client, figure a way to get rid of him fast. If you stay with him, you can pretty much count on the best scenario being you'll get nailed as an accomplice to something you know little or nothing about. Cops or the DEA, maybe the FBI or whoever, will put pressure on you to tell them everything you know, and when you can't tell them what you don't know to begin with, they'll lock you up for three to five years. Or, if you do know something you could use to bargain with, Dennis Dwyer will have you killed before you can tell them anything." He downed the rest of his whiskey and pushed the empty glass across the bar.

"Gee, don't sugar coat it, Louie."

"Just telling you the facts, Dev. Dennis Dwyer doesn't have any friends. I doubt he ever did. It's all about him and always has been, and he's completely comfortable with that. He doesn't need people, well, except to use them, and then he discards them, throws them under the bus, literally or just disposes of them in some other way."

"Sounds charming," I said.

"He either has something he can hang over your head and screw you, something he'll threaten you with to get whatever he wants and screw you, or he'll come across super sweet and then screw you."

"And he's successful operating like that?"

"In a manner of speaking, apples don't fall far from the tree. How 'bout this, the name Mickey O'Connell ring any distant bells with you?"

"O'Connell? You mean that guy that was killed maybe six or seven years ago, shot about a dozen times then cut up into little pieces and they made a pizza out of him or something."

"Close, they actually made sausages out of him, bratwurst, if I recall correctly. Anyway, the guy that supposedly killed him or had him killed was Dennis Dwyer's old man, Sean. He's now serving life in ADX Florence, out in Colorado. I think it's the highest security prison in the U.S., certainly one of the most, if not *the* highest, security prison in the country. Dennis Dwyer is nothing more than a carbon copy of the old man, and that's not a compliment."

"Bratwurst? Man, that's grim. And the old man got nailed for killing Mickey O'Connell?"

"Actually, no, they never got him on that, or anyone else for that matter. To tell the truth, I think when the cops showed up at the packing plant, they looked up and down the street, didn't see anyone who looked guilty, and decided the case was unsolvable. Not sure what they did with the bratwurst."

"Sorry I even asked."

"Yeah, not that Sean Dwyer eventually getting put away for life was any loss to society. Once he was out of the picture, I think local crime statistics were cut in half for about ninety days or so. At least, until the likes of his son and heir apparent, Dennis Dwyer or your close personal friend, Tubby Gustafson started battling it out."

"Yeah, Tubby, don't get me started."

"Funny thing is, Mickey O'Connell had a daughter, a redhead."

"Whatever happened to her? Don't tell me Dennis Dwyer killed her, made her into bacon or something?"

"No, nothing like that, it's even worse. It turns out the lord really does work in strange and mysterious ways, she married Dennis Dwyer."

"You gotta be kidding me? Didn't she know Dwyer's old man made bratwurst out of her father."

"Love at first sight. Or, in that case, maybe it was first bite? I can't recall," Louie said, then laughed and nodded at Mike for another refill.

"I just heard the Dwyer name in a roundabout way, and then the name on the vehicle registration came up. I don't plan on getting anywhere near Dennis Dwyer or any of those folks for that matter, believe me."

Mike slid Louie's fresh drink across the bar, and I threw a twenty down.

"My advice, stay as far away as possible from Dennis Dwyer and his crowd," Louie said.

"Not to worry, I plan on doing just that."

Louie studied me over the rim of his glass but didn't respond.

Twenty-five

I chatted with Mike for a few minutes after Louie left, then said good night and headed out to my car. I'd just closed the driver's door and put my keys in the ignition when a black AMG-63 Mercedes pulled alongside my car, no more than a half-inch away. The rear door was even with my door, and I rolled down my window. The dark-tinted window on the Mercedes was lowered, and Tubby Gustafson took a sip from his martini glass then looked at me. His red nose, the size of a baked potato, hung out of the window.

"Haskell, chasing business away from The Spot, I see."

"Hi, Mr. Gustafson, funny seeing you here."

"And what, exactly, is funny about that?"

"Oh, well, I didn't mean it was funny, exactly, what I meant was that you never—"

"Silencio, Haskell. Bit of advice for you, although God only knows why I would even bother. 666 Lakeshore Drive, a rather unique vehicle you may find interesting."

Dwyers address near Sophie's house.

"Why? What's happening?"

"Better hurry, Haskell," Tubby said, then raised his window, and the Mercedes drove off.

Two hours later, against Louie's wise advice, I was parked about three doors up from Dennis Dwyer's place. The same three vehicles as the other night were parked in the circular drive, a black SUV, a four door Mercedes and that expensive looking red sporty thing I could only dream about owning.

The Mercedes and the sporty thing were parked too close to the SUV to be able to read the license plate. So I had no way of knowing if the SUV was the same one the thugs who stopped me in the parking lot a few hours ago had been driving. I didn't see any point in attempting to climb the brick wall with the wrought iron fence. There was no sign, anywhere, of the white retro Chevy paneled van. Whatever Tubby had been talking about, I'd either missed it, or he'd led me on a wild goose chase.

I checked my watch. It was just after eleven-thirty. I'd been sitting out here for the better part of an hour twiddling my thumbs while trying to make sense of Molly O'Connell marrying Dennis Dwyer after his father, Sean, supposedly served her father up in the form of bratwurst. Never try and figure out people's relationships or taxes, I guess.

I thought some more about Sophie taking on the task of trying to instill basic good behavior in Morton. Unfortunately, I was afraid I had to agree with her. Poor Morton was a product of his environment, namely living with me. Between the hours I kept, and truth be told, my life-style, being raised in a fraternity house would probably be a step up for the guy. It would be interesting to see how things worked out, but as good, kind, and talented as Sophie was, I had my doubts when it came to any hope of success. Morton had become about as irreparable as me.

A first floor light in the Dwyer house suddenly went off, and a half minute later, another one flashed on up on the second floor. By the shape of the window, I pegged the room as a bathroom. A moment later, another light went on in what appeared to be the room next door, then after fifteen minutes, both lights went off almost simultaneously.

I waited another ten minutes just to see if someone came out and hopped in one of the cars, but nothing happened. Finally, I decided to call it a night, as far as the Dwyer's were concerned and headed back into town and my porta pottie office.

Twenty-six

Some idiot had taken my parking place in front of the rambler. So, I parked further up the block, maybe a half dozen doors closer to the railroad tracks. As I approached the tracks, I could see Ozzie's guy out front talking to someone in a car. He seemed to nod then hurried away. I quickly crossed the railroad tracks, unlocked the office door, stepped inside, and locked the door. I was able to record the license plate on the car before they got their order and pulled away.

Our assumptions had been correct, business was heavier than the night before, but then again, this was Thursday night, the new Friday as they called it. The peak in traffic lasted almost an hour longer than the night before, and for the first time, there were two guys running orders and cash to and from Ozzie's house.

Sometimes, the waiting line was four or five cars long, although it seemed to be orderly. People pulled to the curb, turned their lights off, and patiently waited until it was their turn to drive into the cul-de-sac and place their order. Once they had placed their order, they would pull around, wait politely until their order was filled, then head back down the street and around the corner.

As far as I could see, there was never any problem with someone jumping in line, arguing about price or the quality of product.

Once again, not so much as a peep from Daisy's house, and I made a mental note to knock on her door tomorrow afternoon just to make sure she was okay.

Virtually right on time, the white retro Chevy paneled van arrived at four in the morning and headed up the driveway. It had been relatively quiet for the past hour, and I grabbed the padlock, locked the porta pottie, and hurried across the tracks and down the block to my car.

My Honda Accord eventually started after three tries. I drove down to the corner, turned onto the main street, and turned again a few blocks later which brought me across the tracks. I pulled over to the curb at the far corner and waited. Just a few minutes later, the Chevy van stopped at the corner, turned, and headed down the street. I pulled away from the curb and followed at a distance.

Maybe two miles away, it turned down an alley and stopped about halfway down in the middle of the block. I went around the block and waited at the far end of the alley, then followed again at a distance until the van made another stop. All in all, over the course of the next two hours, it made a total of seven stops, all of them on the east side of town. Stops that, I could only assume, had to be product deliveries and cash pickups.

I followed the van back through the downtown area, where it pulled onto West Seventh Street. I let it get further ahead, making sure there were always a couple of cars between our vehicles.

At the three-story brick building I'd scouted out yesterday afternoon, it pulled into the drive that led to the back parking lot. As I drove past, I couldn't see the van anywhere and presumed it had pulled in back and parked.

I drove back to the east side, parked in the space I left two hours ago, then walked up the street to the railroad tracks. I didn't see anyone waiting for their order to be filled. So, after a few minutes, I hurried across the tracks and quickly let myself back into the porta pottie. Wilkes and Devitt arrived about fifteen minutes later.

Once again, they sat in the cab of their truck and appeared to be wolfing down donuts and coffee. I could hear my stomach growling, as I watched for a few minutes then decided I would take the chance. I slipped on a high visibility green vest, stepped out of the porta pottie, walked over to their truck and knocked on the window.

Wilkes jumped at the sound, spilling steaming coffee in his lap. He swore then rolled down his window. Devitt seemed to be laughing.

"Haskell. What the hell do you think you're doing? God, you've probably given me a third-degree burn between my legs," he said then looked over my shoulder for any sort of activity.

"I'm willing to bet that's the most heat you've had there in years. Wondering if you might have a donut to spare? I've been watching the two of you, and my stomach started growling."

"Are you crazy? Do you have any idea what in the hell could—"

"Come on, Wilkes, now you have to give him one. If Ozzie Frick or any of those bastards are watching, we have to make it look like he's working with us."

"No way. You want a donut, take one of Devitt's."

I looked past Wilkes and focused on Devitt for a moment, then looked at the tray with two sugar donuts that rested on his lap.

He just stared back at me and didn't say anything, although the smile had suddenly disappeared from his face.

"Yeah, all of a sudden, it's not so damn funny anymore, is it? For God's sake, you two idiots," Wilkes said, then snatched one of Devitt's sugar donuts and handed it out the window to me.

"Hey, hey, stop. Give that back, Jackass. What the hell do you think you're doing?" Devitt half yelled, then quickly looked around to see if anyone was watching.

"Paying you back," Wilkes said.

"But that was mine."

I immediately took a bite of the doughnut, it felt slightly warm, and the sugar coating had some cinnamon mixed in with it. "God, this is great."

"Yeah, it should be, you didn't have to pay," Devitt said.

I took another bite and pulled my wallet out, took out a crisp five-dollar bill, and tossed it over to Devitt. "That should be enough to cover this one and maybe grab a couple for me tomorrow morning."

Devitt mumbled something I couldn't make out, as he stuffed the five into a front pocket.

"How'd it go last night?" Wilkes asked.

"No real surprises, busier, like we expected. They had two guys running back and forth to the house, filling orders for an hour or so. Delivery van was here around five, right on time."

A car suddenly came up the street and waited, the driver, a guy in a shirt and tie who was probably on his way to the office, looked at us nervously for a long moment, but didn't leave. We continued talking. After a minute or two, one of the guys emerged from behind the hedge and approached the car. He stood on the passenger side and spoke to the guy, keeping an eye on the three of us the entire time. We couldn't make out what was being said, but we had a pretty good idea. After a minute or two, the guy hurried up the driveway to the back of the house.

"You can't make it up," Devitt said and just shook his head.

"Guy's probably a banker or a lawyer," Wilkes said.

"Yeah, with a couple of kids at home. I'd like to get out and kick him in the ass, hard," Devitt said.

“So, other than being busier, everything was normal last night?” Wilkes said.

“Yeah, nothing out of the ordinary, just more of it,” I said. I didn’t want to tell them I’d followed the paneled van all around town in the early morning. In fact, I wasn’t even sure I was going to tell Nelson.

“Well, why don’t you take Devitt’s seat, I’ll drive you over to your car. That’ll work better than you walking back across those railroad tracks or down the street.” He turned to Devitt, “I’ll be back in just a couple of minutes.”

“Here,” Devitt said, handing him the five-dollar bill I’d tossed his way a few minutes earlier. “As long as you’re driving around, maybe get me another sugar donut. I feel like I need some additional fuel.”

Twenty-Seven

On my way home, I swung by my office just to check the mail. Other than a couple of bills, there was nothing of interest. It was probably two or three hours before Louie would wash up on shore. So, I just left him a note saying I'd stopped in and was going home to sleep. Once home, I microwaved two frozen tacos for breakfast and followed that up with a dish of ice cream before heading upstairs to bed. I was just about to fall asleep when my cellphone rang. Sophie.

"Hey, Sophie, how are things going?"

"Seriously, Dev?"

Oh-oh. "What's he done?"

"While I had him in the pantry for his time out, he managed to get into a cupboard and devour an entire box of muesli."

"He actually ate that stuff?"

"And then, as if that wasn't enough, he ate half a loaf of sourdough bread."

"I sort of get the sourdough bread, but muesli? That health food stuff? I can't believe he went for that," I said, although there was a part of me that wasn't really too surprised.

"Not really the point, Dev. I put him downstairs and locked him in the laundry room, thinking that would teach him a lesson."

"Don't tell me he ate the soap."

"No, that would have been poetic justice. Unfortunately, he ate my thongs, absolutely destroyed six of them."

"Well, he comes by that honestly," I said, trying to lighten the mood.

"Really?" she said, apparently not finding any of the humor I'd attempted to interject. "I'll have to go out and buy some more later today."

"How about if I go out to Victoria's Secret later today? I'll get some really nice silky thongs for you."

"I think I can buy my own underwear, Dev. Right now, the last thing I need is you getting involved."

Given the tone, I was tempted to answer, 'Yes ma'am,' but instead, I said, "Gee, I'm really sorry, Sophie. I think I mentioned, left to his own devices, Morton is liable to be trouble. I was gonna grab some sleep, but I could be out there in the next half hour and pick him up. It might be better for all concerned if I came and got him."

"No, it's just his way of upping the game. I'm in the alpha slot here, and he's not going to get me out."

It was beginning to sound like she was suddenly taking Morton's action very personal.

"Look, you don't have to do this, Sophie. Besides, I know how he is. The guy is incorrigible, at best. Let me get out there and get him before he really drives you nuts. God only knows what he plans to do next."

"No, Dev. I think you're giving him too much credit. In fact, it would be best if you were to stay away for at least another day. Right now, he's probably expecting you to show up and rescue him. So, do not come out here, I don't want to see you. You'll just set back what little progress I've been able to make."

"Where is he now?"

"He's taking a time out in Lilly's travel kennel. He can stay there and watch while we go through our daily routine of commands, and she gets rewarded with a treat. Hopefully, he'll begin to see the benefit of good behavior."

"I think you're giving him a little too much credit."

"It's a standard procedure in dog training, Dev. Morton isn't the first delinquent I've had to deal with. You'll see, he'll come around."

She had more faith than I did. "Okay, you certainly know better than I do."

"Thank you."

"I'll give you a call later this afternoon to see how things go."

"I'm sure we'll make progress. Sweet dreams," she said and hung up.

I wasn't sure there was going to be any progress made. After all, we were dealing with Morton. Mr. Stubborn. I drifted off to sleep and dreamt about shopping for Sophie at Victoria's Secret."

Twenty-eight

I woke a little before three that afternoon. I grabbed a shower, had a light lunch of leftover sausage pizza then headed out to check the places the paneled van had stopped at in the early hours of the morning. All I did was drive past the places, wrote down the address, then circled the block and gave each of them a second pass before I headed off to the next one on my list.

I drove down the alley where the van had gone, but I wasn't exactly sure which address it had stopped at so, I added two house numbers to the list. I phoned Lieutenant Nelson when I got back home.

He answered the phone, sounding like my call had interrupted the half dozen things he was doing at that exact moment.

"Nelson," he half-shouted.

"Hi, Lieutenant, Dev Haskell, here."

"What do you need, Haskell?"

"Actually, it's what I have for you."

"Sorry, but if it's something on the images you recorded last night, I've only read the summary. Haven't had a chance to view last night's tape yet."

"No. It's got nothing to do with what's on the tape. By the way, busy night last night, at one point, they had two guys taking orders and four and five cars backed up waiting. I'm thinking tonight will be even busier with the weekend here."

"That's about what we expected to see, although I have to say this location is generating way more business than we initially realized."

"Which might be the reason Daisy was raising hell. It turns out to be one of a number of locations being run by the same group."

"And you know this how, exactly?"

I went on to explain my early morning drive following the paneled van around the east side of town.

"You were supposed to stay put, Haskell. We don't need you getting in the way."

"Working as a non-paid volunteer, I'll take that under advisement, Lieutenant."

"I really don't want you getting any more involved than you already are. Something happens to you, and there's going to be hell to pay."

"And if you shut down this place right now, the business will simply drift to one of the other locations currently operating, and you won't decrease the problem for more than twenty-four hours."

"That's for us to worry about. Right now, your job is to stay put in that porta pottie."

"Yeah, sure, the office, as you call it. Not a problem. I guess I won't pass on this list to you with the addresses to over a half dozen different locations where these guys are running the same sort of business. Why would I even bother? After all, I certainly wouldn't want to be the one responsible for a decrease in Dennis Dwyer's illegal drug business."

"Addresses? How'd you get addresses."

"I did something really unique. After the delivery van departed Ozzie Frick's, I followed it around town for the next hour or two. By the way, during the day, it seems to be parked in the parking lot behind the building at 1035 West Seventh."

"Damn it, Haskell. I thought I gave you strict orders not to go there."

"I didn't go there," I lied. "I just drove past. I got a funny feeling that if you do some checking, you may find out that Dennis Dwyer doesn't just rent an office for that bogus shell company named after his wife. I think he probably owns the entire building. That parking lot is fenced in with an eight-foot fence around it and a roll of concertina wire strung out on top of that, not exactly the sort of thing a real estate or insurance office would need."

"And you know this how?"

"Like I said, I just drove past the place."

"Why were you even driving past?"

"I don't know, maybe because it's only about four blocks from my office and it's located on one of the two main thoroughfares on that side of town. That paneled van along with a black SUV with tinted windows and the two thugs who drive it are in that parking lot."

"You seem to suddenly know a hell of a lot for just driving by the place."

"What can I tell you? They passed me on the street, as I was getting out of my car. There's gotta be only one of those 40's retro paneled vans in the seven-county area, and the thugs in the SUV were right behind it. They drove onto 35E heading south. I'm guessing out to Burnsville and Dennis Dwyer's place."

"Haskell, so help me God, if you go off on another rogue mission and screw up this investigation, there will be hell to pay."

"Oh, no. Please don't fire me. I really need this job. Oh, hey, wait a minute, you can't fire me because I don't work for you. I volunteer, which means I'm not even getting paid. That's why all this time I've been working for free. How are the budget meetings going by the way?"

"Like I don't have enough of a migraine headache, just talking to you."

"Not to worry, Lieutenant, I'll be back there tonight, working for free, I might add."

"Just don't do anything crazy, please." Nelson actually sounded like he was pleading with me.

"About as crazy as I intend to get is having a donut or two with Wilkes and Devitt tomorrow morning."

"I'll be sure to warn them," Nelson said, and then disconnected.

Twenty-nine

I did my usual routine, parking in front of the rambler on the far side of the tracks. Once I got within sight of the porta pottie, I waited until the guy taking orders ran up to the house. There were actually two guys taking orders again, and I'd just made it inside the Porta pottie when the other fellow waved the next car forward. The cars were already waiting three deep, and the order guys were literally running back and forth.

I started recording and kept at it until a little after three before I had a chance to grab one of my cheeseburgers. I also had the feeling that someone, maybe more than one individual, had been using the office for its intended purpose, which did nothing to improve my appetite.

After three, the traffic began to slow down considerably, but it was still heavier than the same time on the previous nights. Another half-hour later, it had slowed down altogether and remained that way. One of the delivery guys appeared to have left. With just a couple of cars every fifteen or twenty minutes, apparently, two guys weren't needed.

While the delivery guy was running an order up to the house a little after three-thirty, I slipped out of the porta pottie. I hurried down by the tracks, climbed up a small bank by the back of the house, and settled into a patch of weeds to watch what happened.

Just like clockwork, the paneled van arrived at almost four on the dot.

He pulled up the driveway then turned around on an asphalt parking area so he would be able to drive back down the driveway. No sooner had he stopped than a guy came out the back door of the house, down some steps, and pulled open the rear door to the van. At the same time, someone with a shaved head hurried out the side door of the triple garage carrying what looked like two canvas cash bags with leather handles, zippered tops, and small padlocks hanging on one end.

The guy at the rear of the van pulled a box out of the back, slammed the door closed with his hip, hurried up the steps, and back inside the house. The guy with the cash bags handed them in through the driver's window and started talking to the driver. I couldn't make out what was being said, but halfway through the conversation, it dawned on me that it was Ozzie Frick standing there. He chatted with the driver for another few minutes, then stepped back, waved, and watched the van pull away before he headed back into the garage, closing the door behind him.

I waited in the weeds for another ten minutes. During that time, the delivery guy from out front by the hedge ran back and went into the garage through the same door Ozzie Frick had used. He was back out in a couple of minutes and took his time walking down the driveway to a waiting customer.

I remained where I was for another couple of minutes and was about to leave when someone walked past me, not more than ten feet from where I was hiding. He wore a baseball cap, a light-colored t-shirt, and jeans. In the grey light just before sunrise, I could make out the pistol stuck into the front of his belt. Fortunately for me, he appeared to either be texting something on his cell-phone or playing a game. Either way, he wasn't paying much attention to anything around him, and I remained still until he was well past me before I slipped back down the bank to the railroad tracks.

I had to wait a good twenty minutes until the delivery guy walked back up the driveway before I hurried back into the porta pottie. Wilkes and Devitt arrived just after eight and proceeded to sit in their truck, drinking coffee and eating donuts.

I waited a few minutes then slipped on my high visibility vest and casually drifted over to their truck. Wilkes lowered his window and handed me a bag without saying a word. I opened the bag and looked in at three sugar donuts. They were still warm from recently coming out of the oven.

"Thanks for getting these, guys. I really appreciate it."

"Anything to keep you away from ours," Devitt said.

"Yeah, besides, Lieutenant Nelson told us you needed a little sweetening, Haskell. Told us we were supposed to keep an eye on you."

"I had some additional information for him, and I guess he was a little surprised I could find my way out of the office over there," I said, giving a nod in the general direction of the porta pottie.

A car headed up the street then slowed down as it drew closer. I could make out two figures in the front seat, but from this distance, it was tough to tell if they were male or female. The car held back for a long moment then backed into a driveway to turn around and headed back down the street.

"I think we just spoiled someone's party plans," Wilkes said, then tossed the last bit of chocolate donut into his mouth.

"Busy last night?" Devitt asked.

"Yeah, two guys running back and forth to the house. Actually, there's a three-car garage back there, and that's where they bring the cash and pick up the drugs. They've got at least one guy patrolling the area back there. Not that he seemed to be paying too much attention."

Wilkes and Devitt looked at one another, then Wilkes said, "You went back there? Are you nuts? You're liable to expose the entire operation, Haskell. We're on thin ice here, as it is. We're going to have to be out of here in the next couple of days. We can only sweep the damn street here so many times before someone with half a brain wonders what in the hell we're doing."

"I wanted to see what was back there. So far, all we've done is record license numbers, not that that does any good. You know the place is busy, you know they're selling drugs, you know this is one of at least seven locations this group is operating. What are you waiting for?"

"Back up for a minute, one of seven locations? Maybe hop in, and you can bring us up to date while we drive you over to your car."

Thirty

We sat in the truck for a good twenty minutes while I told Wilkes and Devitt what I'd seen the morning I followed the paneled van. They didn't say anything all the while I described what I'd done and only made one comment once I'd finished.

"Interesting," Wilkes said.

Devitt just nodded.

So much for feedback. On my drive home, I debated about calling Sophie then decided against it since she'd told me not to. I fried up a pan full of bacon, ate that for breakfast, climbed into bed, and promptly fell asleep. I woke up later that afternoon, still feeling tired, grabbed a shower then headed down to my office. I made a point of driving past the building on West 7th Street where the paneled van had been parked but didn't see anything.

As I stepped into my office, Louie looked up from his picnic table desk and said, "Well, if it isn't the mystery guest, how are things?"

"Tell you the truth. I'm dragging. This working nights is beginning to take a toll."

"You learning anything?"

"Yeah, this Ozzie Frick is doing a hell of a business, and his place is just one of at least seven locations that your friend Dennis Dwyer appears to be running. Matter of fact, I should stop by Daisy's place this afternoon and see how she's doing. I haven't heard anything from her since my first night on this gig."

"She okay?"

"Yeah, at least as far as I know. It just seems sort of strange that she was out there haranguing folks with a bullhorn, and now, we haven't heard so much as a peep from her."

"Maybe she wised up. Ozzie Frick and his pals aren't the sort of crowd you want to piss off, and they're just stupid enough to do something violent."

"Yeah, maybe I—" My cellphone suddenly rang, and I checked the screen, Sophie. "Hey, I better take this, it's Sophie."

"Oh, yeah, she's watching Morton. Good luck," Louie said.

"Sophie, hi. How are things going?" I said, then held my breath waiting for the roof to cave in.

"Just wanted to let you know I think we've turned a major corner. We worked well together for most of the day. He's out in the back garden playing with Lilly right now."

"You're kidding?" I said, not meaning to sound so surprised.

"No, he's been great. Maybe a little short on the attention span, but that's coming around. Another few days, and you won't recognize him."

I couldn't believe she was talking about Morton. "What have you been doing?"

"We're just working on the basics. A few basic commands, walking, of course, we've been working together in the basement for right now, less distraction down there. Another day or two, and we'll move outside."

"I'm not sure what to say, that's fantastic."

"I thought you'd like that. How are things going for you?"

"Oh, man, more of the same. Really dragging right now, I was just telling Louie these night hours are starting to take their toll."

"You're down at your office? Oh, you poor thing. Are you getting enough sleep?"

"Yeah, I think so, but then, when I wake up I'm still feeling tired."

"How much longer are you going to be doing this?"

"I'm not sure. It's one of a number of things that I have to talk to the man in charge about."

"How about if I made you dinner tomorrow night?"

"Oh, you're really nice to offer, but you're already doing so much with Morton."

"I love working with him. Once we settled on who's in charge, it's been a real treat. Why don't you plan on coming over for dinner tonight? I'll whip something up, and we can have a relaxing evening before you go off to work."

"Tell you what, let me pick up a couple of steaks. We can sit out on your deck. I'll grill the steaks, you can do your usual fabulous job with a salad and some other dishes. Sound like a plan?"

"Yeah, sounds like just what the doctor ordered. I'll plan on seeing you around six-thirty. Okay?"

"I'll be there, and thanks for calling with the Morton update, no one is happier or more surprised than me."

"Bye, bye, bye," she said and hung up.

I set my phone on the desk.

"Sounded like good news," Louie said and gave me a surprised look.

"Yeah, Morton's not only behaving, he's also learning manners. I gotta get her some sort of thank you gift."

"What are you thinking of?"

"I'm thinking a diamond."

"A diamond ring? No offense, Dev, but isn't it just a little too soon for that sort of thing?"

"Not a ring, Louie. God, are you kidding? No, I was thinking of a nose stud."

"A what?"

"A nose stud, you know she wears that stud right here," I said, and pointed at my nose.

"And you're going to get a diamond?"

"Yeah, I was in a shop the other week, and they had a half dozen of the things, they even come with a certificate that says they're real diamonds."

"Gee, how could you go wrong if there's a certificate?" he said, sounding more than a little sarcastic.

"Exactly. In fact, if I go now, I could pick it up on the way to Daisy's."

Thirty-one

Pawn America was located out on Rice Street, sort of on the way to Daisy's. If you have an idea of a pawn shop being a grimy place with some old guy just sitting on a stool behind a thick window of bulletproof glass, this wasn't it. It was more like a trendy store with shiny bicycles arranged by the front door and electric guitars hanging on the back wall behind glass counters filled with everything from laptop computers to iPods and jewelry.

Just inside the door was a muscular looking guy with a white earphone in one ear. He was wearing a black suit. The suit coat looked about three sizes too small, and the sleeves around the guy's massive biceps looked like stuffed sausages. He gave me a nod but didn't smile, as I stepped into the store.

I headed over to the jewelry counter. Along with expensive watches, earrings, bracelets, and a couple hundred rings, there were two trays with nose studs, twice as many as I recalled from my visit a couple of weeks back.

"Need some help?" a guy asked. He was standing behind the counter, and his name tag read 'Brad.' He wore a black golf shirt with the red Pawn America logo embroidered on his left breast. His head was shaved along the sides, and long dark hair combed back on top, very trendy.

"I want to look at the nose studs."

"We've got a very nice selection," he said as he unlocked the sliding door to the glass case. He pulled out the two black velvet trays and placed them in front of me. Maybe a third of the studs had stones, and the rest were little designs, including two that were crosses and one that was a silhouette of a naked woman sitting. I'd seen the same design on mud flaps hanging from the back of semi-trucks. All the studs with stones were priced between sixty and eighty-five bucks with one exception.

"How come this one stud is priced at twelve bucks, and the rest are five times more expensive?"

"The others are all diamonds, we even have a certificate of authenticity that goes with them," Brad said, and then flashed a big smile.

"And this one doesn't have a certificate?"

"Right, unfortunately, it's only cubic zirconia, sir. So, no certificate."

"Yeah, and just twelve bucks. I'll take it. Can you put it in one of those little black jewelry boxes?"

"I can, but I'll have to charge you a dollar for the box."

"That's fine. This way, she'll never know the difference," I said.

"I actually have two choices on the box. I can give you the standard black one," he said, reaching into a drawer and placing the box on the counter. "Or, we've got a couple of these," he said and placed a red velvet box in the shape of a heart on the counter. "We've got a couple leftover from Valentine's Day."

"Oh, man, I'll take that red one. Fantastic. You do a lot of business here on Valentine's Day?"

"You wouldn't believe it, almost for a month leading up to the day, then for the week after we have a lot of ladies coming in and umm, pawning the gifts they got. Not uncommon to sell a piece and then see it end up back here two or three days later."

"Sounds kind of depressing."

"Yeah, but it's the business. If that sort of thing really bothers you, you probably shouldn't be working here." Brad placed the nose stud in the center of the heart-shaped jewelry box. It looked like a shiny little crumb. He flashed a quick smile, then said, "Anything else I can help you with today?"

"No, that'll do it for me."

"Cash or credit card, sir."

"Amazingly, I have the cash," I said, then pulled a twenty-dollar bill out of my wallet and handed it to Brad. I was headed out the door two minutes later, carrying a small bag with the red Pawn America logo on it. I ditched the bag in a recycling bin on the corner then stuffed the little red velvet box in my pocket.

Thirty-two

I headed over to Daisy's place. As I drove up her street, I noticed that Wilkes, Devitt and their truck were nowhere to be seen. Daisy's front porch appeared to be empty. I had to park a couple of doors down, then walked up onto her front porch and rang the doorbell. The porch swing was there, but the bullhorn was gone, and the chain that Axel, her dog, had been attached to was coiled up beneath the swing.

I immediately heard Axel begin to bark in response to the doorbell. I could see him a moment later through the beveled glass of the front door window, barking and growling at me. Daisy suddenly appeared behind him, looked at me for a moment, smiled, gave me a wave and opened the front door.

"Axel, no, now don't you bite," she said, then sort of half-closed the door as Axel lunged toward me. "Give him a moment to calm down, and he'll be fine," she said.

Axel's teeth were bared, and he kept barking and lunging.

"Oh, for God's sake, Axel, exactly who do you think you're fooling? We've got company now, you be nice, so I can let Mr. Hassle in."

Axel continued to bark and growl.

"Axel, damn it, I'm not going to tell you again." Axel suddenly stopped barking, sort of sniffed the air, then turned and walked away. "Honestly, some days, I just don't know. Come on in, Mr. Hassle. What brings you here?" she said as she closed the door behind me and headed into her living room.

The room was covered with a dismal grey wallpaper with kind of a faded green design. It looked like it predated the Roosevelt administration, Teddy Roosevelt. The seams where the strips of wallpaper came together had puckered and pulled apart, and a good six-inch section in each corner had curled down from the wall sometime over the past hundred years, revealing a hint of pea soup green wall beneath. From somewhere toward the back of the house, I could hear a mechanical sort of rumble.

"Have a seat," she said and pointed to a worn couch with brown cushions. I sat down in a corner of the couch and sank toward the floor by about a foot so that my knees were almost up level with my chest. Daisy didn't seem to notice.

"What's that rumbling I hear, your furnace?" It was eighty-five degrees outside.

"Oh, no, umm, it's my clothes dryer, I just put a load in."

It sounded like she either had shoes in there banging around or the thing was going to explode. "What do you hear from up at the end of the block?"

"Mmm-mmm, nothing new. A large amount of traffic, especially late at night. Weekends being the worst. Not that anyone seems to care. From what I can tell, I'm just about the only one who cares. The rest around here are almost all renters anyway and apparently can't be bothered."

"But no problems with them threatening you or maybe doing damage to your property."

"No, at least not yet, but it's bound to only be a matter of time. I've given up calling the police, and my council person won't return my phone calls anymore. You'd swear they were on the payroll."

"No damage to your car?"

"No, nothing like that, thankfully. Of course, I do have Axel here to protect me." At which point, Axel came into the room holding a tennis ball in his mouth. He walked over and placed the tennis ball at my feet, backed up a couple of steps, and waited, looking back and forth from me to the tennis ball.

"Go ahead and give it a kick," Daisy said.

"I pretended to kick the ball a couple of times, faking out Axel and getting him to move first to the left and then to the right. I kicked it hard past his left side, and he leaped after the ball, chasing it out into the hallway.

"He'll tire of it in a minute or two. He was napping when you rang the doorbell. He's up a good portion of the night watching the cars out on the street."

"You have a lot of traffic out there at night?"

"You've no idea, especially after midnight. Car after car and the police don't seem to care in the least."

I wanted to tell her that I was out there on stakeout every night this week and that I was fully aware of the traffic and the business that was being conducted, but then what? Hope she wouldn't tell anyone? She'd probably be back on the bullhorn threatening people as they drove up the street yelling that they were heading into a stakeout. Not a very good idea, so I didn't say anything.

There was a long moment of quiet before I said, "Well, I just wanted to stop in and check on you, say hello, make sure everything is okay."

"It's nice of you to stop by," she said, and stood up from her chair, sending the clear message our brief conversation was over.

I had to sort of bounce a couple of times to get out of the couch and stand up. "I can still hear that rumbling sound. You sure your dryer is all right?"

"Oh, yes, it's always like that, just another load of laundry. It never seems to end," she said and smiled.

Axel was lying on the hallway floor with the tennis ball close to his head. He opened an eye as I walked past, but didn't bother to get up.

"See, now he's very comfortable with you, Mr. Hassle. Well, thank you so much for stopping by, nice to see you again," she said, opened the front door, and sort of ushered me out of the house. I had the distinct impression she was anxious to get rid of me, not that I really cared. Everything seemed fine, and maybe she did have some sort of knowledge that Ozzie Frick was under the watchful eye of the cops.

"Nice to see you again, Daisy. Stay safe, and hopefully, things around here will get back to normal."

"Whatever that is," she said, then closed the door behind me.

As I walked back to my car, my phone rang. Lieutenant Nelson.

"Dev Haskell," I answered.

"Haskell, Nelson here. Listen, I've pulled Wilkes and Devitt off the stakeout, and I don't want you going in there tonight."

"Why? What's the problem?"

"Problem? Well, budget for one and the fact that it's the weekend and having a crew in there on a Saturday and Sunday might just raise some eyebrows. Besides, I think we should assess what information we have and come to some decisions. I've got Wilkes and Devitt coming into my office at nine on Monday morning. You're more than welcome to join us."

I was going to suggest I just sneak into the porta pottie tonight like I'd done for the past week then remembered I was doing steaks out at Sophie's tonight and thought it might make perfect sense to extend dinner into a sleepover. Especially since I would be arriving armed with a jeweled nose stud.

"Okay, I understand not going in there tonight. But just so you know, I'm more than willing to do it."

"No, I appreciate the effort, but not necessary," Nelson said.

"I'll plan on joining you on Monday morning, your office."

"Yeah, like I said, nine sharp, see you then."

Thirty-three

I pulled into Sophie's driveway at exactly six-thirty Saturday night. Sophie was already standing at the door wearing a pair of short shorts, a t-shirt touting a 2015 Bob Seger concert in Tampa, and no bra. The evening was shaping up.

"Right on time," she said, holding the door open for me. "Lilly and Morton are out in back playing."

"He's still on his best behavior?"

"He's been very good, Dev. Now, I want to caution you, when you see him, please stay calm, a little rub behind the ears is fine, but do not get him all riled up. Part of our progress is we're remaining calm. He's been wonderfully relaxed today. I'd like to keep it that way."

"Got it," I said. "Calm, that's me tonight."

"Mmm-mmm, can I get you a glass of wine or maybe a beer? Or, I've got some 7-Up if you'd prefer that."

"A beer sounds great."

"You're working tonight?" she said in a tone that suggested I should probably stick with the 7-Up.

"Actually, having dinner with you, steaks on the grill, just some nice conversation instead of being on stakeout all night seemed like such a relaxing change that I phoned the guy in charge and told him I couldn't make it in tonight."

"Really?"

"Yeah, believe me, I need a break."

"Oh, that's so sweet." She gave me a kiss, then took me by the hand and led me into the kitchen. I was ready to toss the steaks on the counter and follow her into the bedroom, but instead, she made a sharp turn and opened up the refrigerator door.

"Maybe get a platter out of the cupboard above the range, and we'll put some salt and pepper on those steaks and let them get to room temperature before you put them on the grill. I'm looking for the beer in here, somewhere," she said, bending over and searching the far recesses of her refrigerator.

I admired the view until she looked over her shoulder at me and said, "Hello. Plenty of time for that later, Dev. Maybe you could get the platter out of the cupboard."

"Oh, yeah. I'm on it. So, Bob Seger," I said, opening the cupboard and pulling out a large platter. "You saw him in Tampa?"

"Yeah, a couple of years back. Talk about work. I think he played for like four hours straight. Probably one of the best concerts I've ever been to. Have you ever seen him?" she said, standing upright and setting the beer bottle on the granite countertop. The cold air from the refrigerator had done its enhancement work on her.

I stared for a moment, hoping she didn't pick up on it, then said. "I like his music, like it a lot, as a matter of fact, but I've never seen him live. I'm really not the concert-going type."

"Oh, I love them, it's just such a great vibe."

"Well, the few concerts I've gone to, the next day I feel I paid way too much for the tickets. I always seem to end up sitting next to some drunk jerk who's intent on singing every song, loudly, and then there's three or four idiots, invariably right in front of me who stand up for the entire show, and I never see the stage. By the end of the night, I just want to hit someone."

She looked at me and just shook her head. "You know, you're right, you probably shouldn't go if they have that sort of effect on you."

I seasoned the steaks while Sophie opened my beer. I'd picked up two meat bones for Morton and Lily at the butcher shop, and I set those next to the meat platter. Then, I walked over to the large picture windows that overlooked the lake. Morton and Lilly were playing in the yard, sort of. Actually, Lilly was sitting with her nose in the air slightly while Morton jumped back and forth in front of her. I sort of got the feeling she wanted nothing to do with whatever activity he was suggesting. Sophie came up alongside me and wrapped her arm around my waist.

"Aren't they playing nicely?"

No point in ruining the evening, so I said, "I can't believe it. It's like he's completely different. If this was last week, he would have figured out a way to dig up your garden and taught Lilly how to hop over your fence. It's like he's a new person."

"Now remember, when you go outside, calm. Keep your voice level."

"Can we bring them those bones?"

"Yeah, but let me carry them. Right now, it's important that he continues to see me as the alpha provider."

"Alpha provider," I said then laughed.

She raised her eyebrows and said, "It can work to your benefit in all sorts of ways."

I got the message and handed her the bones then picked up the platter with the steaks. "You lead the way."

We were halfway across the patio before Morton turned and looked in our direction. He paused for a moment, then gave a happy yelp and ran toward me.

"Come on, buddy, hey Morton, it's so good to see you. Come on, come on."

"Dev, were we not listening? Remember, calmly, calmly," Sophie said.

I set the platter on top of the grill then gave Morton a rub behind his ears. "Good to see you, boy. Did you miss me?"

Sophie set her wine glass on the table, then looked very formally at Morton, cleared her throat, and held her right hand out, palm up, like she was stopping traffic. "Morton," she said.

Morton gave her a look, then seemed to ignore her and jumped back and forth in front of me.

"Morton," Sophie said, this time more forcefully as she held her hand out again. I automatically took a step back.

Morton jumped back and forth a few times, then seemed to get the message and suddenly sat.

"Oh my God, I don't believe it. Sophie, you really have him trained."

"We're just beginning, believe me, there's lots of work left to do. Now, if you'll attend to the grill for a moment."

I took the steak platter off the grill and set it on the table, then raised the lid on the grill and fired it up. Sophie remained in eye contact with Morton then slowly lowered the palm of her hand. Morton immediately laid down. I wanted to comment but didn't.

"Come, Morton," Sophie said, and walked out to the middle of the backyard. She worked with Morton and Lilly giving commands, having them sit, stay and lay down. Lilly was on top of it, Morton, mmm-mmm, not so much, but he was trying, I think.

I called Sophie, about ten minutes later. "Hey, Sophie, I'm going to take these steaks off the grill and let them sit for a few minutes. You want to keep working with those two, and I'll get things out of the kitchen?"

"No, I'll do it. That's enough class time for Morton anyway," she said, then clapped her hands, Lilly immediately went over to her ball. Morton looked at me for a long moment, then went over and started jumping around Lilly.

I helped Sophie carry out the salad and vegetables. She went back into the kitchen, grabbed a bottle and a glass for me. I placed the nose stud in the heart-shaped box beneath her napkin. She set my wine glass on the table, filled my glass, topped up hers, and sat down.

"What's this?" she said, picking up the box with a surprised look on her face as she placed the napkin on her lap.

"Little something for you. I can't believe the job you've done on Morton. Nothing short of amazing."

"Oh, Dev, you didn't have to do this."

"It's a diamond," I lied.

Her eyes grew wide, and she grabbed the box and lifted the lid. "What the . . . Oh, it's, it's a nose stud. How umm, how very nice of you." She smiled, but the smile somehow seemed to have an edge to it. The diamond joke may not have been my best idea.

The steaks were great. I even liked the salad and vegetables. I cleaned my plate. Sophie sort of played with her food, barely got through half her steak, and had three more glasses of wine.

Thirty-four

I was kicking myself as I loaded the dishwasher. After dinner, Sophie had opened another bottle of wine and drank half of that then said she was really tired and went to bed. Stupid, stupid, stupid me. My diamond joke had cast a pall on the rest of the evening and ruined any hopes I'd had of a raucous late night.

Morton was asleep, Lilly was asleep, and I knew Sophie was out like a light because I could hear her snoring in the bedroom upstairs. I finished cleaning up the kitchen, opened another beer, served myself a second piece of blueberry pie, and sat down in front of Netflix. I climbed into bed a little after midnight but didn't have the courage to try and wake Sophie.

I was on my second cup of coffee a little before six the following morning. Everyone was still asleep. I was in my boxers, still mentally kicking myself for the stupid diamond comment I'd made that put a damper on the rest of the night. I was sitting on the couch, staring out the picture windows at the lake. It was foggy again. But the sun coming over the trees looked like it would burn the fog off over the next hour.

I suddenly saw him or thought I did, the ghost clown. Out there in the fog, walking for just a second or two. The red nose and clown makeup, it was him, but then, just as fast, he was gone. I sat there for another half hour staring as the fog gradually disappeared, but I never saw the clown again. I set my coffee mug on the granite counter and decided to go back upstairs to the bedroom to try and see if my luck would be any better this morning. I was halfway up the stairs and casually glanced out the window above the front door when I saw the paneled van drive by, no doubt heading up to Dennis Dwyer's.

I hurried into Sophie's room. She was breathing deeply, still sound asleep. At least, she wasn't snoring. I quickly got dressed, tiptoed out of the room, and hurried out to my car. It started on the second try. I sped out of the driveway and up the street. I slowed as I approached Dennis Dwyer's estate, pulled over, then hurried along the brick wall and peeked in through the wrought iron double gates. The white paneled van was parked behind the black SUV. The red sporty thing was parked at a funny angle in front of the SUV, and the Mercedes in front of that.

The front door of the house suddenly opened and out walked the thug who had driven the van and slowed down to give me a long look in front of The Spot the other day. He had dark, curly hair, combed back like some fifties rock and roller. He wore jeans and a t-shirt with a large red X across the front and some words in black that I couldn't quite make out. He opened the passenger door of the van, then gathered up five of the leather and canvas bank bags just like the one I saw Ozzie Frick hand him the other night. He kicked the van door closed then hurried into the house, closing the door behind him. I waited another ten minutes, but he didn't show, so I got in my car and drove back to Sophie's house.

The front door was locked. I didn't think Sophie had locked me out. She was probably still asleep. In my hurry to get up to Dennis Dwyer's, I forgot the door would automatically lock behind me. I hurried around the back to the patio, but the door leading into the sitting room was locked as well. Morton and Lilly appeared to still be asleep, so rather than wake them, I settled into one of the patio chairs, listened to the birds chirping, and waited for Sophie to wake up.

Morton and Lilly were up about an hour later, but they didn't seem to notice me. They headed upstairs, most likely to Sophie's room, fifteen minutes later they were back downstairs with her. Sophie was wearing the Bob Seger t-shirt, but I thought it best not to ask if she'd slept in it.

"Oh, Dev, what in the world are you doing out here? I thought you left or something."

"No, just cleverly locked myself out of the house."

At the sound of my voice, Morton ran over and placed his head on my lap. I rubbed him behind the ears for a bit then remembered Sophie's cautionary message about remaining calm and not getting him excited. After a moment, he followed Lilly out to the far corner of the backyard.

"Hey, I put some coffee on for you."

"That sounds great. You want a refill?" Sophie said.

"Yeah, but make sure there's enough for you first. I think my mug is sitting on the kitchen counter."

She was back a minute later and handed me my coffee mug. "When did you get up?"

"Oh, I think I woke up a little after five. My sleep schedule has been all screwed up ever since I started working nights."

"That police business you're doing?"

"Yeah, I'm there around midnight and home around nine the next morning."

"God, I'm so glad we don't have that sort of thing out here. It's one of the reasons I moved to the burbs, just a nice quiet neighborhood with people minding their own business and obeying the law."

I wanted to say something about her neighbor's the Dwyer's, Dennis, and Molly but decided it maybe wouldn't be the best move.

"Notice anything?" Sophie said.

"You're not wearing anything underneath?"

"No, you perv, look." She tilted her head toward me. The cubic zirconia nose stud was attached. "Diamonds are a girl's best friend," she said and smiled.

God help me if she ever got the thing appraised. "You like it? I think it looks great on you," I said.

"Yeah, thanks, I'm sorry if I was crabby last night. It was really nice of you to get this."

"You weren't crabby, you were probably just tired, and the bottle and a half of wine you had maybe didn't help."

"Yeah, I suppose. You feel like coming back for dinner tonight. I promise not to be crabby, well, as long as you don't say or do something completely stupid."

"I don't know, maybe. What are you having for dinner?"

She gave me a look.

"Kidding, just kidding. With any luck, I'll be finished with the case I've been working on so I can make it, and I'd love to."

"You think they're not going to do it anymore?"

"Yeah, I got a very strong feeling they're getting ready to wind it down."

"That would be fine with me. To tell you the truth, I didn't want to say anything, but I've been worried about you."

"Oh, thanks, that's nice."

She suddenly looked at me, sort of bit her lower lip, and said, "You know, I really don't want to wait until tonight. Maybe finish that coffee, and I'll race you upstairs."

"Actually, I think I've had enough coffee," I said and set my mug on the table.

Thirty-five

Following a couple of hours of very personal attention from Sophie, I was back at my place by mid-afternoon. Sophie had decided I didn't need to return that evening which was just fine with me. I needed the rest. I did a load of laundry, put together a dinner of leftovers, finished off a tub of frozen yogurt while watching a movie, and went to bed at a decent hour.

After a healthy breakfast of eggs and bacon, I was waiting in the lobby of the police station for someone to escort me up to the meeting in Nelson's office. Devitt walked in the front door, not too long after I took a seat in the lobby.

"Haskell, you here for the meeting up in Nelson's office?"

"Yeah, they were going to send someone down to escort me up."

"Come on, you can ride up with me. Jerry," he said to the sergeant behind the desk. "Let 'em know Haskell is coming up with me, and they don't have to send anyone down." The sergeant nodded as Devitt punched in a code on the keypad next to a grey metal door. Once he heard the lock click on the other side, he held the door open for me. "We can hop on that elevator. I don't feel like taking the stairs today."

We were seated in a conference room just down the hall from Nelson's office a few minutes later. Myself, Devitt, Nelson, Aaron LaZelle, two other guys from narcotics whose names I'd already forgotten and just to round things off, my arch enemy and ruler of the evil empire, Detective Norris Manning. We were waiting for Wilkes to show up.

At five minutes past nine, Nelson said, "All right, screw it, let's get started." He proceeded to give a rundown of the activity we'd recorded over the past week. "We've got everything from what we could call recreational users to hardcore addicts showing up here. Based on the recordings gathered, we've got close to ten percent, making a minimum of five repeat visits within a twenty-four hour period. Vehicle registrations are across all walks of life and income levels. We," he stopped as the door to the conference room opened, and Detective Wilkes stepped in carrying a white box. "How nice of you to find time to join us, Detective."

"Sorry for the delay, some woman ahead of me was ordering a wedding cake of all things. God save me. Here," he said, opening the box and revealing three rows of different types of donuts. "Figured this group could use more than a little sweetening." He set the box on the end of the table, and everyone immediately jumped out of their seat and grabbed a donut.

Nelson grabbed a chocolate donut then settled back into his chair. He took a bite then set the donut to the side on a section of paper towel. "We've sent some undercover folks in at night. There seem to be three products available, in order of dollar value they are cocaine, then ecstasy and finally, weed."

"And these are being supplied on a daily basis?" one of the detectives, whose name I'd forgotten, asked.

"Inventory delivered and cash receipts picked up every morning around four like clockwork. This is one of seven operations. We believe they're all part of the Dwyer organization." A couple of looks were exchanged, at the mention of Dwyer's name.

"I can add a little bit to that," I said.

"Oh?" Nelson said.

"The cash pick up, and the product delivery is made in a white paneled retro 40's Chevy van."

"The license number is in your handouts along with an image," Nelson said.

A couple of people turned a page on the handout Nelson had provided.

"Gee, not what I would call subtle," someone said, looking at the picture of the paneled van. "Talk about not blending in, what the hell are they thinking?"

"I happened to be out in Burnsville, on personal business Sunday morning," I said. "That vehicle drove to the Dwyer estate just a little after six in the morning, pulled into the Dwyer estate, then proceeded to unload seven bags that I believe were filled with the night's cash receipts from the various Dwyer locations."

"Damn it, Haskell. You were snooping around Dwyer's house. I thought I told you not to get involved."

"Actually, I was out there on personal business and saw the paneled van drive past. It's gotta be the only vehicle like that in the seven-county metro area. I drove a short distance to Dwyer's place, saw the driver carry the money bags into the house, and I left. I didn't confront anyone. I didn't make any noise, I wasn't seen."

"But you could have been. You could have blown this whole effort," Nelson said.

"Sorry, thought the information would prove useful. If nothing else, it would seem to establish the fact that Ozzie Frick is the first stop on the route."

"And you know this how?"

"Seven stops, including Frick's, and the guy is hauling seven bags of cash out of the van bright and early Sunday morning, theoretically at the end of what is their busiest night of the week."

"You may find this difficult to grasp, Dev," Aaron said. "But we'd come to that conclusion some time ago. While I can appreciate your effort and the confirmation it lends to our decisions, I have to agree with Lieutenant Nelson. No offense here, and we certainly appreciate the fact that you've graciously volunteered, but that doesn't mean you're automatically privy to all we're doing on this particular operation," Aaron said.

"We'll maybe have a little chat after our meeting, just you and me," Nelson said.

Devitt flashed me a quick smile then focused on the handout Nelson had provided. The meeting went on for another thirty minutes. At the end, Nelson looked around the room and said, "I think we can move to the next phase immediately. We're going to shut down all seven locals, simultaneously, tomorrow morning. The key will be shutting this Ozzie Frick site down before the delivery vehicle arrives so that we can secure the site, then grab the vehicle and driver as well. Lieutenant LaZelle and I will be working out the details for that operation over the course of the morning. Let's plan on meeting in the assembly area again this afternoon at four. In the meantime, go home, try and get some sleep, we're going to have a busy night ahead of us and stay safe."

"Just a question," I said. "Wouldn't it make sense to wait until the weekend when there's more activity?"

Nelson exhaled and seemed to pause for a moment looking for the right words. "Actually, no, it wouldn't. We could nab a bunch of the buying public next Saturday, but you'll be looking at a series of minor possession charges at best, not to mention the fact if there's trouble, if these dealers put up a fight or try and shoot their way out, it would simply be a lot safer, for everyone, if there were fewer bystanders around."

With that, everyone pushed away from the table and headed out the door. Just about everyone, except Aaron LaZelle, grabbed another donut on the way out.

“When you’re done talking to Nelson, stop down in my office,” Aaron said, then left.

Thirty-six

When it was just Nelson and me in the conference room, Nelson looked at me and shook his head, then tossed a pen onto the table and said, "Haskell, what the hell part of keep a low profile and don't get involved do you not understand?"

"I told you, nothing happened, it was early in the morning, very early. No one was around. It's not like I climbed the wall then crawled beneath the paneled van or anything. I just watched from a distance, outside the six-foot high brick wall Dwyer has all along the property. I barely peeked around the corner. One of the thugs I saw a few days before came out of the house, pulled seven bags out of the front seat of the van, and went back inside the Dwyer house. It probably took me longer just now to describe it than it took him to actually haul the bags into the house. I hung around a few minutes longer. Nothing happened, so I went back to my friend's house, that's all, end of story. No one drove past. No one was looking out the window. No one saw me. No one knows I was even there, well, with the exception of you and the other guys that were in this meeting."

Nelson shook his head. "Do not, under any circumstances, go anywhere near the Dwyer home, Ozzie Frick's place, or the office building down on West Seventh Street today. Do I make myself clear?"

"Yeah, sure thing, not a problem. I would still like to be a part of the action tonight."

"You think you can follow directions? Keep a low profile and stay in the background? Because I gotta tell you, I don't need anyone thinking they can't wait any longer and then deciding they're going to lead the charge."

"Yeah, I'll behave, I promise."

"Here's what you're going to do, if we decide to let you participate at all."

"I'll do whatever you want, I promise."

"We'll see about that. If we decide you can join us, you will be restricted to staying in the office."

"That porta pottie?"

"Right, your office. You'll be in there doing just what you've been doing on any other night. Recording the vehicles as they come and go. Anything unusual, any vehicle going up that driveway, or for that matter leaving via that driveway, we'll want to know about it. Can you do that?"

"I was sort of thinking, maybe being with one of the teams going in."

"Not that you wouldn't be an asset, but no. For a variety of reasons, not the least of which is your own safety, not to mention that of our teams going in. This isn't like the movies, Haskell. This is damn dangerous work. You saw that armed individual when you were lying in the weeds the other night. He won't be the only one out there looking to protect that enterprise."

"The porta pottie? Really?"

"That's it or nothing. Let me just add, if you don't want to do that, I understand, and I thank you for the work and effort you've put in this far. But, we need someone in there tonight to make sure things are going to be relatively like what we've prepared for. If you're not there, I'll have to pull someone off one of the teams going in. I'm sure I don't have to explain the potential problem that can present. So, porta pottie or nothing," Nelson said, then smiled.

"Okay, I guess I'm in the porta pottie."

"Thanks, I appreciate it. I'll see you in the assembly area at four."

"See you then," I said. I left the conference room and headed down the hall to Aaron's office.

Thirty-seven

As I rounded the corner heading into the Homicide office, I could see Detective Manning talking to Aaron. Aaron was leaning against the door frame of his office, and Manning had his back to me. It looked like Aaron was giving Manning instructions on something. I didn't feel the need to approach until Manning was out of there.

A guy nearby looked up from his desk and said, "Can I help you?" He gave a nod at the yellow visitor's badge clipped to my belt.

"Just waiting to speak with Lieutenant LaZelle over there. I'll wait until he's finished with Detective Manning."

The guy spun halfway round in his desk chair, looked at Aaron and Manning for a moment, then nodded and sort of lifted his chin at the chair alongside his desk. "Probably be a good idea. Might as well grab a seat. Looks like it may be a while."

I sat down in the chair and tried to stare off in the distance and appear preoccupied. He didn't seem to be buying it.

"I know you from somewhere?"

"My name's Haskell, Dev Haskell. I'm working on something with Lieutenant LaZelle and Lieutenant Nelson."

"Haskell? You that guy they have locked in that shit house over on the east side?"

I had to laugh and nodded. "Yeah, it's something like that. I'm on the midnight to eight shift. No rest for the wicked as they say."

"Yeah, I remember one time having to spend the better part of a week in the back stall of a ladies' room."

"Sounds interesting."

"Believe me, it wasn't. Everyone else was out in the main barroom, chatting all the ladies up. I had to listen to, well, let's just say it wasn't the best place to be and leave it at that."

Manning finally headed off down the hallway. "Looks like the Lieutenant is free, I better grab him while I can? Thanks for the chair."

"Not a problem, thanks for helping us out."

Aaron watched me approach for a moment then waved me into his office as he turned and went in. As I stepped into the office, he pointed to a chair in front of his desk. "You okay with Nelson?" he said.

"Yeah, I can go tonight, just as long as I remain confined in the porta pottie."

"Probably the best place for you. I hope you understand. It's all about safety for both you and our teams. Something ever happened to you, Dev, Nelson and I would be kicked off the force before sunrise. The powers that be have no idea you're going to be there or that you've been helping out. God, if they did, there would be hell to pay. That said, we need someone to keep an eye on things up to the time we're ready to move in. Who better to do that than the guy who's been working the night shifts for the past week. You've more experience than anyone else in that department, so it will keep you safe and keeps us informed at the same time."

"Yeah, I suppose. It's just that, I don't know, it's like I'm a pain in the ass."

"Well, yeah, of course you are, but that's never stopped you before. Look, the goal here is to shut down Ozzie Frick's little enterprise along with a half dozen other places Dennis Dwyer has been operating. You're playing a part in that, an important part. Enough said."

"I suppose. Anything else?"

"No, just wanted to make sure you were on board, it will really help, Dev and it's much appreciated."

"Yeah, thanks, Mr. Sensitive, I'm fine. See you at the meeting this afternoon."

"See you at four, now, let me get to work, we've got a lot to hammer out between now and then."

Thirty-eight

I went over to my office and checked the mail. Two offers from the same cable company, another offer from American Express, and a notice from my bank that a client's check for two hundred dollars that I'd deposited had bounced twice. Cyril Highmen.

I picked up my phone and called my client, Cyril. Make that my former client. The recorded message said the phone had been disconnected, and no other number was available at this time. Great.

Two hundred bucks was not the end of the world, thankfully. But two hundred bucks was two hundred bucks. I left Louie a note saying that I'd stopped in and gone through my mail and that it looked like my nighttime gigs were just about finished. Then I headed over to Cyril's office.

Highmen Investments maintained a small, store-front office on Selby Avenue. The office was close enough to my house that I could have walked there in fifteen minutes, but since I was coming from my office, I drove. I pulled up directly in front of the door, which maybe told me something, available parking signaling perhaps a lack of business.

Looking through the front window, I could see a wooden desk that looked like it had been rescued from a dumpster. Two beige metal folding chairs with the local high school's name stenciled across the back sat in front of the desk. A crumpled paper bag that appeared to be from McDonalds was the only item on top of the desk.

There was an 'Office For Rent' sign leaning against the inside of the window. The typed notice taped to the front door was even less promising. The notice was actually from the landlord stating that the locks had been changed and if Cyril wanted access to his office, he could call the number listed below and bring his rent current within the next fourteen days. I called the number.

"Citywide Properties," a pleasant voice answered.

"Hi, I'm standing outside of Cyril Highmen's office at 967 Selby Avenue. There's a notice on the door that suggests he's out of business, and I'm wondering if someone in your office might have some information."

"What was that address?"

I repeated the address, heard some key's clicking on a keyboard, then she said, "Oh, my. Stella Benedict is handling that listing. Just a moment, please, while I transfer your call."

After two rings, a sugary voice answered and said, "This is Stella. How may I help you?"

"Hi, sorry to bother you, Stella. I'm actually looking for Cyril Highmen. In fact, I'm standing in front of his former office right now, and there's a for rent sign in the window with a notice taped to the door that says the locks have been changed. Can you tell me how I can get in touch with him?"

"I'm afraid I didn't catch your name."

"Haskell, Dev Haskell. Cyril was a client of mine."

"A client?" she said, obviously waiting for more information. I really didn't have any.

"Yes, a client."

"I'm afraid I've no way of contacting him. If I had a means of contacting Mr. Highmen, I would gladly pass it on. We've not received any response to our phone calls, and personal attempts to contact him. He seems to have literally disappeared."

"Does he owe you rent?" I said, asking the obvious.

"I'm afraid I'm unable to respond to that question. It goes against our privacy policy."

Interesting response since they had no problem broadcasting that fact to the neighborhood. "Well, for your records, I've attempted to deposit a payment he sent me, and the check has bounced twice. I'm sure it's a much smaller amount than whatever his monthly rent would be."

"Oh, I'm sorry to hear that. Honestly, if I knew of a way to contact him, I would pass it on, but, like I said, he seems to have disappeared, vanished."

I gave her my phone number, and we promised one another we'd be in touch if we learned anything. I suspected Citywide properties was out a lot more than two hundred bucks. It probably cost them that much just to have the locks changed, not to mention a month or two for rent.

I phoned Sophie next and left a message. She returned my call before I made the five-minute drive home.

"Hi, Sophie," I answered.

"Hi, Dev. Sorry I missed your call. Funny you called. I was just about to call you to see if you wanted to come over tonight. It's just leftovers, but I was thinking we could maybe celebrate if you're finishing up this police project you've been on. Morton and I have been working most of the morning on heel and stay."

"How's he doing?"

"We're coming along, slow but sure."

Poor Morton, I thought. "Listen, I won't keep you. I would love to swing by tonight, but it looks like I've got one more night on this case, and then I'm finished."

"This is the police thingy?"

"Yeah. They're going to shut things down tonight. So, I'm almost done."

"Well, you know how I feel. I won't be sorry to see you finish with that. It really worries me."

"Relax, there's nothing to worry about, honest. Can I get a rain check on tonight's celebration?"

"Yes, of course. This will just give us another day to bring Morton's behavior to perfection. You'll be very proud of him."

"Looking forward to it, Sophie. Sorry if I messed up your dinner plans."

"I'll just call B.B. and invite her over. She's always fun."

"Well, say hi to her for me and have a fun night. Thanks again for all the work you've done with Morton. I'll talk to you tomorrow."

"You just take care and don't do anything crazy. You know how you can get."

"I'll be on my best behavior."

"You do that, and there might be the opportunity for some misbehavior when you're here."

"Exactly what I was hoping," I said, and we hung up.

Thirty-nine

I was sitting in the assembly area, actually a large basement room, with Aaron, Lieutenant Nelson, Wilkes, Devitt, and about twenty other guys. Nelson was going over the operation planned for later tonight. They planned to move in on Ozzie Frick's property at two forty-five in the morning then wait for the white paneled van to arrive. My job was to lock myself in the porta pottie and remain there until someone told me it was safe to come out.

The mood in the room was serious, and you could feel the tension in the air. Everyone was paying attention. Some were taking occasional notes, no one was talking or making funny comments. The meeting went on until almost seven, at which time we were set free until ten when we had to report back.

Wilkes and Devitt were kind enough to invite me to join them for dinner over at Mickey's Diner. The place is actually a historic site in town. It was designed to look like a 1930's railroad dining car. It's been serving meals twenty-four hours a day, three hundred and sixty-five days a year for the past seventy years. I'd been there before, with mixed results, once I almost didn't make it home in time before I lost the chili I'd eaten. Rather than repeat that chili incident tonight and then lock myself in the porta pottie for five or six hours, I ordered a bacon cheeseburger and a strawberry malt.

While we waited for our food to arrive, Wilkes asked, "So, what do you think?"

"What do I think? This has always been an okay joint. I had the chili last time I was here and loved it, but it didn't like me. I almost didn't make it home."

He and Devitt shook their heads, and Wilkes said, "Hey, dumb shit, I was talking about the operation we're going to be on in a couple of hours. God. What do you think about the plan?"

"Oh, yeah. Well, I just want everything to go smoothly. Be nice to have this entire drug operation finally shut down so I can get back to some sort of normal in my schedule. Be even better if we could nail Dwyer," I said.

"What makes you think we won't?" Devitt said.

"It's not like he's been moving this stuff himself. The product is usually delivered around four in the morning. The cash is picked up from Ozzie and a half dozen joints and hauled out to his estate. I saw it happen yesterday morning with that idiot in the paneled van. But we're just shutting down Ozzie Frick's place and then grabbing the van."

"Yeah," Wilkes said. "And what do you think is happening with the paneled van after that?"

"I suppose you'll hang onto it and keep it as evidence or something."

Devitt laughed. "Haskell, it's our ticket into all the other locations. We'll convince the driver to lead us to the remaining locations and then back to Dwyer's. Don't worry, we'll get your man." He glanced at his watch. "Twelve hours from now, he'll be under arrest and probably all lawyered up. End of story, and with any luck, we'll all be headed home safe and sound."

"Oh, I guess I never really thought of that bit. I was afraid they were just shutting down Ozzie and then hoping to get information on the other sites."

"Well, don't tell anyone you heard it from us."

Even though Devitt knew three of the folks on staff at Mickey's, service wasn't the fastest, so we didn't get out of there until a little after nine. We headed back to the station in Devitt's car. All three of us were focused on what was going down over the next few hours, so the car was quiet.

Once back at the station, we headed down into the basement assembly. Everyone was dressed in black, including me. We all had protective vests. The SWAT guys carried helmets. I'd probably looked at my watch a dozen times in the past five minutes and at one point, actually put it up to my ear to see if the thing was ticking. We definitely seemed to be in the 'hurry up and wait' mode.

Finally, at eleven-forty, I got the nod from Nelson to head out. What little conversation there was stopped, as I headed out of the room. I got a couple of pats on the back, Wilkes yelled, “Stay safe, Haskell,” and I was on my way.

Forty

I was going to play it just like I had every other night for the preceding week. Park a block away on the far side of the tracks, slip into my porta pottie office, and begin recording. I'd been given a small field radio in the event something didn't seem right. I could communicate verbally or send a text message just like a cell phone.

I drove over to the east side and parked in front of the same house like I'd done most of the nights. As I walked up the block toward the railroad tracks, I saw the same kid I'd seen the first night sleeping on the couch with the TV on. Tonight he looked wide awake and appeared to be clicking the remote every few seconds.

I crossed the railroad tracks then crouched down in the weeds. There was a car turned around in the cul-de-sac with its headlights off, although I could hear the engine running, and the driver's foot was on the brake pedal illuminating the brake lights. I waited for at least five minutes, but nothing happened. No one came out to the car to take an order or make a delivery. Eventually, the headlights were turned back on, and the car headed down the street and around the corner.

A few minutes later, another car drove up the street and stopped. I had to duck down because the headlights were shining in the general area where I had been waiting. I moved over maybe twenty feet and waited in the weeds, but it was more of the same. No one came over to the car and took an order. After close to ten minutes, the car turned around in the cul-de-sac and headed back down the street.

I moved back across the railroad tracks and walked partway down the block, then got on the radio and called Nelson. Nothing happened. I tried to reach him a couple more times before it dawned on me that he was probably still at the station with everyone else and out of range. I called him on my cell phone but ended up leaving a message. The number I had was for his office phone, exactly where he wouldn't be. I phoned Aaron and unfortunately got the same results.

I walked back to the railroad tracks, crossed over, and waited in the weeds for what seemed like an hour. I finally got tired of waiting, crouched down, and hurried over to the porta pottie with the key in my hand. I quickly stood to unlock the door just as a pair of headlights swung onto the street and hurried up toward the cul-de-sac.

I reached for the padlock, only to discover it wasn't there. The car was getting closer, and I had to decide whether to step inside or hurry back to the weeds. The door had always been locked before, and it wouldn't be like Wilkes and Devitt to forget. Something was wrong, and there was a strong possibility someone had been in there. Maybe they were in there even now, just waiting for me. I stepped away from the porta pottie and hurried back into the weeds. No sooner had I ducked down than the car turned around in the cul-de-sac, passing its headlights over me and screeched to a halt. I could make out two guys in the front and one sitting in the back of the car. After a minute or two, another guy suddenly popped up in the middle of the backseat, and a moment after that a woman sat up. She appeared to be blonde and brushed a strand of hair away from her face. Some sort of conversation transpired. I could see her shaking her head no, then suddenly the rear passenger door swung open and she hurried out of the car.

She somehow looked familiar, although, with the large sunglasses she was wearing at this hour, it was hard to tell. She was dressed in a sort of bikini top that was tied around her neck but untied in the back. She wore short, cutoff jeans that appeared unbuttoned and unzipped. Her blonde hair was sort of arranged in a bun on top of her head, although a few strands appeared to have come undone. She leaned back into the car, said something I couldn't make out, then hurried toward the porta pottie.

"Hey, get your ass back here," the driver yelled.

"I just told you, you're next, so wait for me. This'll only take a minute," she shouted over her shoulder and kept moving.

Forty-one

I ducked down as she drew closer to the tracks. Another male voice suddenly shouted from the car, "Hey, bitch, you want to get paid?" as the porta pottie door squeaked open and then closed behind her.

Once I heard her voice, it suddenly dawned on me who she was, but the explosion a moment later made me duck down, cover my head with my hands and push my face into the dirt. Plastic bits of porta pottie and it's contents rained down a second later.

It sounded like someone swore, and I was vaguely aware of the car in the cul-de-sac burning rubber as it accelerated down the street and skidded around the corner.

I heard some high pitched screeching and popped my head up. I could just make out the blonde figure standing there, screaming something unintelligible. She was shaking her arms then ran the back of her hands over her eyes and mouth. Her sunglasses and the bikini top were gone, with the exception of a small strap hanging around her neck. The bun on the top of her head had disappeared and in it's place was hair that appeared to hang limp and wet, as if she'd just stepped out of the shower.

I hurried over to her as she stood there screeching, and waving her arms.

"Eeew, eeew, eeew."

I was about ten feet away when the smell hit me. Unmentionable slimy bits and remnants of toilet tissue, the contents of the porta pottie, covered her body. I instinctively recoiled and said, "Swindle Lawless, is that you?"

"Oh, God, get this shit off me, get it off," she screamed then waved her arms around, flinging more bits in my general direction.

I took a couple of steps back and said, "Calm down, Swindle, and stop shaking your arms, for God's sake."

A voice yelled something from behind the hedge and then fired a shot at us.

Swindle screamed, started to run, then slipped in a pool of porta pottie residue and fell to the ground with an audible splash.

I jumped to the side, pulled a pistol from the back of my belt, and fired back.

I don't know if I hit whoever had been shooting, but he didn't fire again. Shouts suddenly sounded from up at Ozzie's house. I pulled Swindle up by the remnant of the bikini top around her neck and dragged her toward the weeds along the railroad tracks. We waited for a moment while I frantically looked around for someplace safer to hide.

Swindle continued to cough and spit. "Oh shit," she groaned.

I wrinkled my nose at the smell and tried not to breathe. “Man, you aren’t kidding. Whew, God, that is really bad.”

She crawled over a few feet on all fours, whimpering and frantically wiping her hands across a patch of long grass. All the while saying, “Eeew, eeew, eeew.” She scraped across her eyes with her fingertips, flinging more bits in my direction.

“Swindle, damn it, watch what the hell you’re doing.”

She blinked in my direction. “Dick Hassle?”

“Close, Swindle. It’s Dev Haskell. Come on, we gotta get out of here, or they’re going to kill us.”

“I can’t go anywhere looking like this.”

A shot suddenly rang out from the side of Ozzie’s house. There was no way anyone could have seen us from up there, but I didn’t intend to wait around. I took Swindle by her slippery hand and dragged her down to the tracks and along the weeds moving away from Ozzie’s house. I could see lights coming on in a number of houses along both sides of the street.

A couple of figures were now standing in the cul-de-sac. They all appeared to be armed. I tried the radio again. It was worthless. I took my phone out and called 911.

After three rings a voice answered, “Ramsey County Emergency Services.”

“Help, shots fired, officer down,” I whispered, thinking if that didn’t get their attention, nothing would.

One of the guys standing out in the cul-de-sac sort of looked around, and I was afraid he might have heard me. I began to drag Swindle further back. We crouched down and moved along the base of a backyard hedge. Fortunately, she moved along quietly, scrapping bits and pieces, off her skin as we hurried toward the far end of the hedge.

"Ramsey County Emergency Services?" the voice said again.

"God damn it, help. Shots fired. Officer down."

"Where are you calling from, sir?"

"I'm on the east side, contact Lieutenant Nelson or LaZelle. There's an operation planned for tonight, but there's been an explosion, and now there's wounded. Please, send help."

Two guys suddenly appeared along the railroad tracks, about where I was when the explosion occurred. They were definitely armed and looked up and down the tracks. They didn't appear to be in any hurry. I clicked my phone off, leaned into the hedge, and pulled Swindle in as far as I could without snapping branches.

A motion detector light flashed on along the side of Ozzie's house, as two more guys came into view walking down the hill toward the cul-de-sac. It looked like they might be carrying MAC-10's.

The guys down near the railroad tracks, there were three of them now, crossed over to the far side of the tracks. They turned and started walking up the tracks, away from us, all the while looking toward Ozzie's house.

Swindle continued to spit and flick unmentionable bits from her body.

I kept wondering where in the hell the cops were, all the while trying not to breathe.

We remained still for a couple of minutes until a motion detector light suddenly flashed on in the backyard on the other side of the hedge. I saw two pairs of feet heading across the yard toward the far corner where we were hiding.

I heard something click, and a back gate swung open. The wooden gate was about shoulder height, and a guy suddenly appeared. At least his head did. He looked down the tracks in the opposite direction. He couldn't have been more than four feet from us. I raised my pistol and took aim.

Suddenly in the distance, a siren could be heard. Whoever was with the guy said something, they slammed the gate closed behind them and ran back the way they came.

The three guys across the tracks hurried up the bank toward Ozzie's house and disappeared. I heard engines starting, and a moment later, what sounded like cars racing away. We stayed where we were. I kept looking toward the cul-de-sac, ready to shoot at anyone who appeared.

Swindle placed a finger against one nostril and blew a couple of times, then placed a finger against the other nostril and repeated the process.

A minute or two later, I could hear sirens racing up the street. Thankfully, more than one. As the vehicles pulled into the cul-de-sac, red and blue lights bounced off the far side of the railroad tracks and the houses beyond. I waited until the motion detector light on the side of Ozzie's house flashed on, and I could see a crowd of figures storming up the driveway, wearing what looked like SWAT team uniforms. More squad cars and a large van pulled up the street on the far side of the railroad tracks, and a moment later, what looked like another SWAT team in helmets charged across the tracks and up toward Ozzie's. I saw Aaron crossing the tracks behind them, it looked like Manning, and someone else was with him.

"Aaron, Aaron," I called, and he turned, crouched, and pointed a pistol in my general direction.

"Don't shoot, don't shoot. It's Dev."

"Dev?"

"Over here, we got wounded."

All three ran over. "Jesus Christ," Aaron said, then sniffed audibly, waved a hand in front of his nose, and took a step or two back. "Oh, man. You all right? What the hell happened?"

Manning and the other guy wrinkled their noses, and Manning made an awful face. "God, Haskell, couldn't you wait? What the hell did you have for dinner."

Aaron looked at Swindle and then raised his eyebrows at me.

"Oh, Aaron, this is Swindle Lawless, umm, an acquaintance of mine."

"Get me the hell out of here, please. I'm covered in shit," Swindle said.

Manning was already on the radio. I think I heard him say, "The house across the street, alongside the railroad tracks. Two down, hurry."

Forty-two

I was standing under a hot shower, Ozzie Frick's shower, as a matter of fact. Aaron LaZelle and Lieutenant Nelson were leaning against the bathroom sink and the door frame, respectively. Wilkes and Devitt had been in a moment before to give us the word. No one had been arrested. No drugs or money had been found. "You guys didn't find anything? Not a trace? I don't believe it."

Devitt had taken the time to joke I had a shitty taste in girlfriends, apparently referring to Swindle.

After her shower, Swindle Lawless had been wrapped in a terrycloth robe that someone had found in Ozzie's closet, then confined to a bedroom.

Once she was cleaned up, Aaron had recognized her from his time working vice, but said, "There's no point in arresting her. On what charge, exactly? Unlawfully entering a porta pottie?"

"Damn it, someone got the word to them, and they left this place spotless, not so much as a trace," Nelson said.

"You check the garage? The night I was in the bushes watching, Ozzie brought the bank bag out of the garage. The guy who was running back and forth filling orders went into the garage to grab the merchandise."

"Yeah, we've been through it," Nelson said, not sounding any too happy. "Pretty much about what you'd expect to find in a garage, paint cans, lawnmower, some garden tools. Some of the guys are still in there going through things. God, first the budget hassles and now this operation, coming up with a big fat nothing. We are so screwed," Nelson said.

I turned off the shower and opened the glass door.

Aaron handed me a towel then turned around so he wouldn't have to watch me dry off.

"How the hell could they know we were coming?" I said.

"Here's my question to you, Haskell. Why the hell didn't you go into that porta pottie? Why did what's her name?" Nelson said.

"Swindle Lawless."

"Yeah. Why did she go in there, and you didn't?"

"She went in there because she had to use it. She was in a car with four guys, working."

"Working?" Nelson said, obviously not following.

"She's a working girl, Lieutenant. The car pulled in to make a buy, she jumps out of the backseat, yells something to them like she'll be right back. Tells one of them she'll take care of him when she returns and then the next thing you know, she's literally in the middle of a shit storm. Those for me?" I said, pointing to a pair of jeans, a button-down shirt, and a pair of red socks with candy canes stitched along the side piled on the end of the vanity.

"Yeah, no point in climbing back into that stuff you were wearing. And Ozzie's not going to miss them," Aaron said.

"Might as well burn what I was wearing."

"You still haven't told me why in the hell you didn't open the door," Nelson said. He was grasping at straws, but I really couldn't blame him. The cost of the operation, in man-hours alone, was a major headache now made even worse by zero results. Reporting to superiors was not going to be a very pleasant task in the morning.

"I was all set to enter, but the door wasn't locked. Wilkes and Devitt have been religious about putting that padlock on the thing. I even had my key out to unlock it. I couldn't believe they forgot, and I figured someone probably cut the lock. The car with Swindle in it was coming up the street. It never occurred to me the thing would be rigged. To tell you the truth, I was afraid someone was sitting in there waiting to put a bullet in my head, so I hurried back into the weeds."

"And you didn't think to contact us?"

"Actually, I tried to. But the radio you gave me was no good, couldn't reach you. I called both of you on my cellphone and ended up leaving a message. All I had for you was your office number. I left a message there. Aaron, you should have a message on your office phone along with your cell. I'm guessing you had the cell turned off for the operation."

"Shit," they both said. Nelson shook his head like he couldn't believe things could get any worse.

I pulled on the jeans, the waist fit, but the legs were about three inches too long. I rolled the cuffs up twice then picked up the button-down shirt. It was light blue with black buttons and a navy blue monogram on the pocket, 'OFF.' I didn't know if that was supposed to be a joke, or maybe Ozzie Frick's middle name was Frank, or Fred, or something. The shirt felt like it might be silk, and I was thinking of maybe hanging on to it until I saw that the sleeves extended down to my fingernails. I rolled the sleeves up to above my elbow, then sat down on the toilet and slipped on the pair of red Christmas socks.

"Come on, let's take a look around," Aaron said. We stepped out into the hallway and headed for the stairs. We passed three bedrooms. Two of them had a pair of guys going through the drawers and closets wearing blue latex gloves. The third bedroom, smaller than the other two, had a full-sized bed positioned up against the wall. Swindle Lawless in the terrycloth robe and a female officer were sitting next to one another on the bed watching tv.

Downstairs, teams were going through virtually every room in the house. Couches were overturned, and two drug-sniffing dogs were being led around. Three large plastic evidence envelopes were stacked up next to the front door. Each one held a pistol. I could make out what looked like a Mark 4 Ruger with the distinctive red logo on the handgrip resting in one of the envelopes.

"Take a good look at what we've recovered so far," Aaron said and shook his head. "Close to twenty-five individuals tearing this place apart, and we basically come up empty-handed. God, there's going to be hell to pay tomorrow morning. Come on, let's check out back."

Forty-three

I followed Aaron out the backdoor in stocking feet. We walked down the back steps and onto the paved area where I'd seen Ozzie hand the bank bag into the driver's window of the paneled van. Three guys with flashlights sweeping across the lawn walked past.

"This is where the van stopped, and over there is where I saw the guy walking security. I was hiding in the weeds just down the bank, and he walked right past, never really paid much attention."

Aaron gave a quick look, shook his head again, and headed for the three stall garage. All three overhead doors were open, and the lights were on. At first glance, it looked like any normal garage, except that the walls appeared to be sheetrocked and painted white. A couple cans of paint, miscellaneous garden tools, and snow shovels hung on the wall. A riding lawnmower was parked in a back corner of the middle stall with a pretty heavy-duty snow blower sitting next to it.

The concrete floors in each stall had been sealed and looked clean enough that you could eat off of them with the exception of a 4-foot x 8-foot sheet of half-inch plywood lying on the floor of the middle stall. The plywood had a large black oil stain in the middle of it, apparently from a car engine leaking oil. The sheet of plywood was screwed into the concrete floor so it wouldn't move. The back wall in the middle stall had a neatly organized workbench with maybe two dozen wrenches hanging in an orderly arrangement based on size. An air compressor stood alongside the workbench, and an overhead heater hung from the ceiling joists. What looked like a small computer sat on a corner of the workbench, and a brown leather recliner was in the corner. The stalls were connected by interior metal doors.

Aaron headed toward the middle stall, where a half dozen guys were standing in front of the workbench. As we joined them, we saw a half dozen monitor screens stacked three across, providing a 360 degree view of the garage exterior.

"Jesus, pretty incredible security for a garage," Aaron said.

"Check this out, LT," one of the SWAT guys said and walked over to a wall and knocked on it. He wore subdued sergeant stripes on his black SWAT team uniform, and his knuckles made a hollow sort of metallic sound when he knocked on the wall.

"What the hell?"

"It's half-inch steel. The walls are lined with this stuff in all three stalls. The doors leading to the other stalls are solid steel. Damn garage is a fortress."

"Something was going on, that's for damn sure."

“Yeah, and check this out,” the sergeant said, and flicked a switch on the small computer. A police broadcast suddenly came across, a squad car reporting a stalled car at an intersection on Robert street was in the process of requesting a tow vehicle.

“They’re tuned into our scanners?” Aaron said.

“Why not? It’s not against the law. I’m guessing they’d know everything that was happening within ten miles of this place, at any time, day or night.”

“So, how in the hell did they get everything out of here? If this place was operating the way we think it was, it should have taken a week to get it cleaned out. No crime in having a police scanner or security cameras, so they didn’t worry about that stuff. See what other bands they have on that scanner.”

One of the SWAT guys shook his head, grabbed his helmet from the workbench, muttered something under his breath, and headed back toward the house. His boots gave off a hollow sound as he walked across the sheet of plywood. Everyone was focused on the scanner, listening for a moment to routine broadcasts between squad cars and the station.

There was a battery-operated drill hanging beneath the wrenches. A black plastic case rested on the workbench just under the drill. I opened the case. It had maybe seventy or eighty different items, masonry bits, wood bits, screw bits, including Phillips bits. The SWAT guy standing next to me glanced over at the open case, shook his head, and shot a disgusted look in my direction. The sergeant started talking to the group, telling everyone to keep the results of the operation, in this case, the lack of results, quiet.

I pulled the battery operated drill off the wall and inserted one of the Phillips bits then walked over to the sheet of plywood. There were eight blue screws holding the sheet of plywood in place, each with a flat head Phillips drive. I pulled the trigger on the drill, it worked. I pushed a button just above the trigger to set the thing in reverse, set the bit in the screw and reversed it out of the sheet of plywood. After the second screw was removed, the sergeant stopped talking and looked over at me.

"Hey, slick, what the hell do you think you're doing?"

I didn't bother to answer and reversed two more screws out of the plywood sheet. They looked about an inch and a half long.

"Dev, damn it," Aaron said. "Quit screwing around, we've got enough headaches here, as it is."

I reversed another screw out. "Yeah, that's what I'm doing, Aaron. I'm goofing around," I said, then reversed another screw out.

"What an asshole," someone said.

"Hey, LT," the sergeant said. "I'm not sure why, but we came up empty-handed, somethings awfully wrong, it's the middle of the damn night and with all due respect, your pal ain't really helping right now."

I reversed another screw out, fixed the bit into the final screw and looked up just as the sergeant tossed his helmet onto the workbench and stepped toward me. “God damn it. When I say something, you better damn well listen.”

I reversed the last screw out, stepped back and pushed the sheet of plywood about six inches with my foot. The sergeant was growing more red-faced with every step.

“Better hold it there, Sarge, or you’re liable to get hurt.”

“Dev,” Aaron shouted.

“Bring it on you little prick,” the sergeant said and reached for me.

I pushed him back, and shoved the plywood again with my foot, it moved another six inches.“Careful,” I said and nodded at the opening beneath the sheet of plywood.

The sergeant glanced at the plywood and grew wide-eyed. He reached down, picked up the end of the plywood sheet, and pushed it back about six feet, exposing a metal staircase leading down to another level. “What in the hell? Hey, check this out, fellas.”

Forty-four

Five guys hurriedly strapped their helmets on and hustled down the steps as the sergeant growled, "Get down there and check that shit out."

The guy in the lead raised his hand when he reached the bottom of the steps, and everybody stopped, lined up behind him on the steps. One guy was still standing at the edge of the opening, waiting to get onto the steps.

The lead guy reached over and flicked on a light switch next to a doorway. A light blinked a couple of times then suddenly flashed on. "Police, everybody on the ground," he yelled and charged into the doorway.

Everyone hurried down the steps and charged down the hallway behind him with their weapons aimed. The Sergeant hurried past me and ran down the steps, picking up the call, "Police, everybody down on the ground, on the ground."

Aaron had his pistol out and waited at the top of the stairs.

"You going down there?"

"Let's wait until they get it cleared. Better step back just in case there's someone down there who tries to make a break for it," he said, and pulled me back from the staircase. “Nice work, Dev, man,” Aaron said, shaking his head. He stretched his neck to peek down the staircase in an attempt to see through the doorway.

“Yeah, not bad for an asshole.”

Aaron looked at me and smiled. “What can I say? Apparently, your reputation precedes you.”

“The sergeant poked his head out of the doorway a minute or two later and called up. “Hey LT, I think we hit pay dirt. Maybe grab Lieutenant Nelson and come on down here. Nice job, Haskell, I take back a few of the things the other guys were saying about you,” he said, smiled and disappeared back down the hall.

“You go on down there, Aaron. I’ll go find Nelson,” I said.

I didn’t have to say it twice. He was down the metal stairs and through the doorway before I headed back into the house. I found Nelson in the kitchen. He was in the process of dumping the contents of a silverware drawer onto the kitchen floor then kicking the contents across the floor. Based on the mess scattered across the floor, it wasn’t the first drawer he’d searched. Not so amazingly, no one else was in the room with him.

“Hey, Lieutenant,” I called from the doorway.

“Not now, damn it. I’m busy searching for some shred of evidence,” he said, not bothering to look up. He kicked a pile of silverware scattering it in about a dozen different directions, bouncing some of it off a distant wall.

"They found something out in the garage they want you to take a look at."

"What?" he said, finally looking up at me. He was red-faced, breathing heavily, and beads of sweat glistened around his receding hairline.

"Something out in the garage. Sergeant said they hit pay dirt."

"Jesus Christ," he shouted, then hurried toward the door slipping twice on broken plates and kitchen utensils scattered across the floor, almost falling in his haste to make it out to the garage. He pushed me aside as he ran out the door and hurried across the paved area into the center garage. I followed him out the door and heard him shout a loud "Whoop," as he disappeared down the metal stairs.

I had to wait for two guys to come up the stairs before I went down. The metal stairs looked like a miniature version of the stairs they roll up to an airplane in rural airports. They were painted a dark blue with handrails on both sides of the perforated steel steps. They were steep, as I headed down, and I grabbed onto one of the handrails and it wobbled slightly. The paint on the treads appeared to be worn from repeated use.

The door was just to the left at the bottom of the steps, and I entered a hallway. There was a damp concrete sort of smell in the air. A string of bare light bulbs was strung in the middle of the hall ceiling and ran the length of the hall, maybe twenty-five feet. The hallway walls were cinderblock and painted white. Three doorways were on the left side of the hallway.

I passed the first door, which led into a small room with a desk and a laptop computer. Two guys were in there going through the desk, and some three-ring binders lined up on the shelf. Their weapons were lying on the top of the desk. A calendar displaying a naked woman hung on one of the walls.

The middle room had three guys standing in it. One was writing down information in a small spiral notebook while the other two were calling out contents arranged on shelves, bottles of pills and what looked like bricks of cocaine lined the shelves. I stood in the doorway for a moment, and the guy with the notebook looked up at me.

"Nelson and LaZelle are in the next room," he nodded toward the end of the hallway. "Take a look, but maybe don't go in there. They got the crime scene team on the way. Hey, nice work, man."

One of the other guys looked over at me, smiled, and gave me the thumbs up.

I walked down to the end of the hall and the last room. Aaron and Nelson were standing just inside the door, in the midst of a quiet discussion.

As I stepped into the doorway, Aaron looked up and said, "Don't come in here, Dev. Don't touch anything out there."

The room had a couple of flat screens mounted on the wall. One of them displayed six different views of the outside perimeter from the security cameras. There was a white-topped plastic table with a desk chair behind it. The table had a pistol resting on it, just off to the side next to some computer printouts. The chair was on wheels and had been pushed back against the cinderblock wall. A large blood splatter was sprayed across the wall. A body lay face down on the floor in a pool of blood, almost in a fetal position. The body had a shaved head, and a large amount of cash was scattered around the body, suggesting he might have been holding it when he was shot. Most of the cash was blood-soaked.

"Ozzie Frisk," Nelson said.

Forty-five

I was only down in the lower level of the garage for a minute or two when Aaron and Nelson moved all of us out and back upstairs, reminding everyone on the way out to be careful not to touch anything. We were all standing in the middle garage stall, patting one another on the back and giving each other high fives when the BCA van pulled up in front of the garage just a few minutes later.

The van was black with gold lettering on the side that read, Crime Scene Team, and beyond that a silhouette of the state of Minnesota and the letters BCA. It was a large van, actually industrial sized and after a moment three people climbed out, two men and a woman. One of the guys stretched, rubbed his eyes as if he was just waking up and then looked around, it was a little after four in the morning.

Aaron and Nelson walked over and began talking to them, nodding in response to some of the things they said. A moment later, we were ushered out of the middle garage stall while the three BCA people began to climb into white hazmat suits. They grabbed what looked like packs from a side door on the van, and Nelson led them back down the metal staircase.

Aaron stood off to the side, alone for the moment, and I walked over to him. "What do you think the deal is with Ozzie Frick?"

"I think someone shot him," he said.

"Gee, really."

"Could be anything, someone got pissed off, or jealous, or even made a mistake. Who knows?"

"What's it mean for you guys?"

"Time will tell," Aaron said with a shrug. "Short term, this site is closed down. They're in the process of raiding the other places, as we speak. So far, nothing's come across, but we'll see what turns up. At worst, it's going to prove a lousy day for Dennis Dwyer. At best, maybe we're able to link the activity to him. It's just a huge load off our shoulders that we actually came up with something here. If this thing had been a bust, there was going to be hell to pay. Thanks again."

"One of the benefits of not paying attention. The sergeant was saying something, and I wasn't listening, watching one of your guys walk across that sheet of plywood, and it just sounded wrong."

"Thank God for attention deficit syndrome," Aaron said.

"Yeah, and it's not even my best feature."

We twiddled our thumbs for another couple of hours. The two SWAT teams had climbed back in their vans and left. Some higher up, whose name I should have known, but couldn't remember, arrived on scene a little after seven. Aaron and Nelson gave him a brief tour of the house and let him look down the stairs into the lower garage level, but the crime scene team was still working down there, and so, it was off limits. He gave a thumbs up and pats on the back to Aaron and Nelson, shouted a "well done," to the few people within earshot, then got in his car and drove off.

We watched as his car headed back down the street, then Nelson shook his head, said something to Aaron, and they both laughed. A good part of the 'coming up empty-handed' stress now being replaced by another kind of stress. At least, this one seemed to be on a more positive note.

A few minutes later, Swindle Lawless was led out of the house, Aaron started to give her a brief lecture that she'd probably already heard a dozen times in her life. She cut him off in mid-sentence and told him she was going to sue the city for leaving an exploding porta pottie on the street. Life being what it was, she'd probably get some shyster lawyer who would win the case and then keep all the money that was awarded to her.

She was barefoot and still wearing Ozzie Frick's white terrycloth bathrobe, although she'd loosened it to almost, but not quite, expose herself. A couple of guys stopped their conversation and stared. She carried a green plastic trash bag containing her porta pottie drenched clothes. The bag was sealed with a knot, and she held it at arm's length until she tossed it in the trunk then climbed into the backseat of the squad car. As they drove past, she put a hand to the side of her head signaling a phone, mouthed the words, "Call me," then slowly ran her tongue over her upper lip. Some things never change.

"Going to need your statement this morning," Aaron said as I watched the squad car with Swindle slow down at the end of the driveway, turn and disappear around the corner.

"How 'bout I just phone it in?"

"No, sorry, but I don't think that'll work."

"It can't wait until later this afternoon or better yet, tomorrow?"

"Nope, 'fraid not. Tell you what, though. You want to head out and change into your own clothes? I'll meet you down at the station in about ninety minutes. Might even be talked into buying you breakfast."

"You're kidding? You buy?"

"Yeah, provided you show up to give your statement, so I don't have to lock you up overnight with a couple of extremely undesirable types looking for a jailhouse virgin."

"How can I refuse when you put it that way?"

"Ninety minutes, and you'll be there?"

"Wouldn't miss the opportunity," I said and then gave a big yawn.

Aaron nodded and said, "I know how you feel. Let me get someone to give you a lift over to your car. That was you parked across the tracks and down toward the end of the block, wasn't it?"

"Yeah," I said, surprised he had caught sight of my car.

"Hard to miss an ugly pink car."

Forty-Six

I pulled up in front of my place, turned the car off and yawned. I looked at the empty house and wished Morton had been waiting for me at the front window. At least I was finished with the midnight to eight gigs so I could bring him home and begin to get my life back to some sense of normal. I figured I'd give my statement, let Aaron buy me breakfast, then sleep all afternoon and head over to Sophie's tonight for some much needed special attention.

My phone rang just as I was stepping into the house.

"Dev?"

"Hey, Sophie, I was just thinking of you."

"You need to come out here, right away."

Morton, no doubt. "Why? What's he done?"

"You, you just need to come out here. Right away, Dev, get out here, please." She sounded like she was crying at this point.

"Sophie, calm down, just tell me what he's done. I have to go down to the police station and give them a statement, shouldn't take more than maybe an hour or two, and I can be out there right after that."

"No, no, that's not going to work. Are you listening? I need you out here, now," she half screamed.

"Look, Sophie."

"Dev," she screamed, "Get out here, please."

"Sophie? Sophie? Hello?" I called her back. After four rings I got dumped into her message center. I figured Aaron's statement was going to have to wait, and I hopped back in my car and drove out to Sophie's. I tried to keep it at just ten miles per hour above the speed limit, but I constantly had to take my foot off the gas. As I raced along the interstate I called her a half-dozen times, always with the same result, getting dumped into her voice mail. To suggest something wasn't right was an understatement.

I waited at the top of the exit off the interstate, looked both ways, and blew through the red light making a lefthand turn and heading for her street. I screeched around the corner, picked up speed heading down her street, and pulled into her driveway.

I parked alongside B.B.'s car, the blue BMW, with the red convertible top. It was pulled up in front of the garage door. The backseat had some sort of designer duffle bag in it. If Sophie called B.B., something must be really wrong. I wondered if Morton or Lilly had been hurt. I rang the doorbell, then kept ringing it another half-dozen times before I heard the lock snap open.

B.B. stood in the doorway, holding a wine glass. "Well, Dev, wow, that was really fast and look at you, costume party?" she said, and laughed, taking in the outfit I was wearing.

"Where's Sophie, is she all right?" I said, stepping past her.

"She's out in the kitchen, go ahead, see for yourself. She's fine. At least, as fine as can be expected under the circumstances," she said, and then sort of giggled.

I hurried out to the kitchen. Sophie was sitting on a kitchen stool with her back to me. I could see her shoulders shaking as she silently cried. An untouched wine glass sat on the kitchen counter in front of her. It wasn't even nine. I looked out in the backyard, Morton and Lilly seemed to be sleeping in the shade. The backdoor was open, Morton raised his head, and sort of glanced in my direction then laid his head back down.

"Sophie? You okay? What's wrong? What happened?" I said. I wrapped my arms around her shoulders and kissed her softly on the cheek. Her eyes were puffy from crying, and she sniffled.

"Well now, isn't that just sweet. Aren't you the perfect gentleman," the voice said. I half jumped as a guy stepped around the corner from the refrigerator. He was neatly dressed in dark trousers and a starched blue shirt with a white collar, the top two buttons on the shirt were undone. A heavy gold chain hung around his neck. His dark hair was neatly trimmed with just the slightest hint of grey around the temples. He held a black pistol in his right hand which was casually pointed at the two of us.

The thing looked large, made even more so by the silencer screwed onto the barrel. The silencer was flat black, eight-sided and was as long as the entire pistol. I couldn't tell what kind of pistol it was, other than dangerous, particularly when pointed at me.

"How very nice of you to join us, Haskell, so we can finally meet."

B.B. laughed and took a slurpy sip of wine.

Sophie began to visibly shake. Tears ran down her cheeks.

"Hey, look, I don't know who you are, or what we're supposed to have done, but I'm sure we can work something out. Why don't you let Sophie go, and we can see about making things right for you?"

"Little late for all of that now. Because of you, I'm out of business."

It suddenly dawned on me. "You're Dennis Dwyer?"

"You're so smart, Haskell. I believe you've already met my wife, Molly?"

I looked over at B.B., who raised her wine glass to me and giggled some more.

"Your wife? Molly?" I said, unable to hide the surprise in my voice.

"Fortunately, we were able to clear everything out before you arrived with the pigs. The fact that you're here suggests we somehow miscalculated, and you missed the little present we had waiting for you."

"The bomb?"

"Most perceptive. Not bad considering you work for that lard ass Tubby Gustafson. You have to be beyond stupid to align yourself with that low life."

"Tubby? I don't work for Tubby. I was trying to help a woman who lived on the street. Believe me, if I'd known that was in any way connected to you or your wife," I nodded in B.B.'s direction. "I wouldn't have been involved, honest."

"You know, Haskell, I actually believe you because I know you're just plain too damn stupid to figure most things out. No doubt thinking you were helping that Daisy bitch when all along Tubby was playing you like a fiddle." He shook his head, glanced at his watch, and motioned B.B. over to him.

She drained her wine glass, set it on the end of the kitchen counter and walked next to him. He wrapped his arm around her shoulder, all the while keeping the gun pointed at Sophie and me.

Forty-Seven

Dwyer said, "Much as I'd like to discuss the finer facts of recent events with you, we, unfortunately, don't have that kind of time. Let's say we all step out back, and you two can join the dogs."

With the mention of Morton and Lilly, Sophie quickly slipped off the kitchen stool.

"Go ahead, Sophie, see how they're doing out there," Dwyer said and then laughed.

Sophie gave me a quick look then ran for the door, calling Lilly's name.

"You too, Haskell," Dwyer said and waved the pistol in the general direction of the door. "Go on outside. Maybe kneel down by those damn dogs. You try anything cute, I'll shoot Sophie. BB, darling, you should go start the car. I'll be out in just a moment."

I raised my hands up about shoulder level. "Look, Dwyer, maybe just leave and get your ass out of town, you don't need a murder rap. They'll never stop looking, you leave now, and you can just disappear."

"Yeah, I suppose you'd like that. But no, I don't think so. Now, move. Come on, get your ass outside."

I kept my hands up and moved toward the open door. Sophie had run over to Lilly and was kneeling down next to her, softly stroking Lilly's side, crying. Morton tried to raise his head for a moment, but he didn't get up, and it suddenly dawned on me that they hadn't been sleeping.

"Lilly, oh Lilly, baby," Sophie cried while she knelt on the grass next to Lilly. Morton attempted to raise his head again, but only for the briefest of moments before it went back down.

"Dwyer. You, you shot my dog?"

"Jesus, Haskell, might I suggest you have a little bigger problem than your damn dog right now," he said and poked me hard in the back with the pistol.

Lilly suddenly moved her hind leg.

"She's still alive," Sophie screamed.

"Not for long," Dwyer yelled and started to laugh just as I spun around and tried to knock the pistol out of his hand. He hung on, but I'd surprised him, caught him off guard, and he staggered forward a half step. I held onto the pistol and slammed my elbow into the bridge of his nose a couple of times.

He grunted as blood spurted onto his fancy shirt. The pistol fired twice, sounding like someone spitting. I swept my leg behind his feet, lifting him up and slamming him onto the stone patio. The pistol fired again. I heard something zip past my left ear, and he released his grip.

I suddenly had the pistol in my left hand, and his eyes grew wide. I took a step back into a two-handed stance and aimed at his knee.

"No, no, don't," he half-shouted, just as I pulled the trigger.

"Dev," Sophie yelled as I hurried back through the house and out the front door.

B.B. was sitting behind the wheel of the BMW. The engine was running, and the radio was playing. By the time she looked up and focused on me, it was too late. Her smile disappeared as I tore open the car door and shouted, "Get your ass out of the car. Keep your hands where I can see them. Come on, damn it, move, get out now, or so help me, you're dead."

She seemed to pause for a moment, and I grabbed her by the hair on the back of her head and pulled. She cried out as I pulled her from the driver's seat and onto the driveway. I kicked her in the rear a couple of times, forcing her to crawl across the driveway, then reached in and grabbed the keys.

"Dennis? What did you do to my Dennis?"

"Back in the house, come on, go."

She gave a funny sort of whine and hurried back into the house.

"Out in the back yard, go, go," I shouted.

She hurried into the kitchen, saw Dwyer rolling from side to side on the patio, gave a short scream, and ran outside. "Dennis, Dennis, baby," she cried, and knelt down beside him. Both her knees were scraped and bleeding. Blood from his knee was pooling on the patio.

"Better pull his belt off and make a tourniquet."

"You, you shot him, you shot him."

I ignored her and ran over to Sophie, cradling Lilly. "We have to get her to the doctor," she said. Morton looked up at me and whined. They'd both been shot, and my first thought was to go over and finish the Dwyer's off.

"I'm calling 911," I said.

"There isn't time, I'm going to bring them to the vet, she's only a few blocks away."

"But 911," I said, and pulled my phone out.

"Dev, they'll take care of Dennis first. Lilly doesn't have that kind of time. You carry Morton out to my car," she said, scooping Lilly into her arms and hurrying back into the house.

I picked up Morton and followed her.

"But what about, Dennis? Dennis is hurt," B.B. cried as we hurried past.

Forty-eight

We hurried into the attached garage. Sophie had the rear door to her car open.

"B.B.'s parked in front of the garage put Lilly in her car," I said, then pressed the button that raised the garage door. Sophie hurried over to the BMW, tore open the rear door and carefully laid Lilly in the backseat. With the Louis Vuitton duffle bag in the backseat, there wasn't room for Morton.

"Here, take these," I said, handing her the keys to the BMW. "I'll follow you in my car."

Sophie grabbed the keys and slid behind the wheel of the BMW. I laid Morton in the backseat of my car as Sophie reversed out of the driveway. She clipped a section of hedge, ran over part of the lawn, bounced across the curb and skidded to a stop. She threw the car into drive and screeched down the street, picking up speed, fortunately, there was no oncoming traffic or kids.

I jumped behind the wheel and took off after her. She sort of slowed at a corner, glanced left and right, leaned on the horn, and blew through the stoplight picking up speed. Thank God, there was no cross traffic, as I slowed down then did the same, flooring the car in an effort to catch up. I pulled my phone out and called Aaron just as Morton gave off a sort of high pitched whine from the backseat.

“When are you coming down?” was how Aaron answered.

“Can’t, on the way to the hospital.”

“What?”

“Dennis Dwyer and his wife are at Sophie’s. I shot him. He was going to kill Sophie and me. He’s laying out on her patio in back.”

“What?”

“Her house is in Burnsville, on Frontier Lane, her backyard looks out onto Alimagnet lake,” I shouted. “Gotta go,” and hung up.

I turned the corner Sophie had fishtailed around just in time to see her bounce over the curb, tear across the lawn of the veterinarian office, and skid to a stop. She was lifting Lilly out of the backseat as I pulled up the drive and stopped. I picked Morton up out of the backseat and carried him in, running to catch up to Sophie.

“Ma'am, ma’am, excuse me, ma’am, you can’t go in there. No, sir, you’ll have to wait,” the receptionist called as we hurried across the lobby carrying the dogs and barreled through the swinging door.

Sophie hurried down the hallway, calling, “Gail, Gail, we need your help here, Gail, emergency. Gail, help me. Gail.”

A woman in a white lab coat stepped out of a room down the hall with a confused look on her face. Her eyes grew wide as she focused on Sophie carrying Lilly and then me carrying Morton right behind Sophie.

"Sophie, bring her in here," she said and hurried across the hallway into another room. "Put Lilly down on the examination table," she said, then looked at me and pointed to the desk. "Move that laptop and lay him down on the desk. What happened?" she asked Sophie.

"They were shot."

"Shot?" She said, taking a stethoscope from a pocket in her lab coat and listening for a heartbeat on Lilly.

Sophie glanced at a large clock hanging from the wall. "Both of them were shot, close to an hour ago."

"It was a handgun, I think a nine millimeter, but I can't be sure," I said.

Gail picked up the receiver on the phone attached to the wall, pushed three keys, waited a moment, and said, "Dr. Myer, Carol, theatre one, stat." Her voice went out over a loudspeaker. She hung up, stepped over to Morton and did the same quick exam. A moment later, a woman dressed in blue hospital scrubs hurried into the room.

"What happened?" she said, seeing the two dogs.

Gail had stepped back over to Lilly. "Gunshots, we're going to start with Lilly here. When Tom gets here, we'll move Morton to the other theatre."

At which point, a young-looking guy in a lab coat stepped into the room. He took a quick look around. Gail held a syringe in her hand, squirted some of the contents out then gave Lilly an injection.

"Tom, we've got two gunshot wounds, the Retriever is Morton?" She glanced at me and I nodded. "Looks like a chest wound, take him into theatre two. I'm going to start on Lilly, here." She rattled off a number of things I couldn't understand, and the guy hurried out of the room. He was back a half-minute later with a small sort of gurney and carefully lifted Morton onto it then wheeled him out of the room. I looked at Sophie, but she was focused on Lilly, and I hurried out the door to catch up to Morton.

We were in another operating theatre, similar to the one we'd just left. The doc wheeled Morton next to an operating table with lots of lights overhead. He carefully lifted Morton off the gurney. I wheeled the gurney over to a far corner.

"I'm Tom Myer," he said, then gave me a slight nod and turned his full attention to Morton. He gave him a sedative, I guessed similar to the injection Lilly had received, but I didn't really know and figured now was not the time to bother the doctor with a bunch of questions. After maybe fifteen minutes, Morton appeared to be asleep, and he took out a pair of clippers and trimmed the area around the wound.

When he finished, he looked over at me and said, "You're lucky, he's going to be fine. I got a call into one of our staff. She's on her way in and," he looked at the door as a dark-haired woman hurried in. "Here she is now. Gunshot wound," he said to her, "he's sedated. Mr.

Morton, if you'll take a seat out in the waiting room, I'll be out just as soon as I can. Kelly, we're going to need . . ." he began to rattle off a list of items to the nurse, and I figured, probably the best thing I could do would be to get out of their way. I stepped out of the operating theatre and headed back down the hall toward the waiting room. The door to the room where I'd left Lilly and Sophie was closed. I paused for a moment, didn't hear anything from inside then continued out to the waiting room.

Forty-nine

As I sat down in the waiting room, the receptionist seated behind the counter gave me a less than positive look but didn't say anything. A rather heavy-set woman with short, uncombed hair and a soiled, light blue pullover top sat maybe three chairs away from me. She held a small white dog on her lap. The woman whispered to the dog continuously while the little white dog eyed me suspiciously. After a few minutes, I stepped outside and phoned Aaron.

"Where in the hell are you?" was how he answered.

"I'm at the vet's office. That asshole Dennis Dwyer shot Morton and Sophie's dog, Lilly. He was going to kill us. Please, tell me you contacted the Burnsville police."

"Actually, I'm out in Burnsville at the house now. Paramedics are just loading Dwyer up to take him to the hospital. Nice aim, by the way, you nailed his knee cap."

"Bastard's lucky I didn't put a round between his eyes. Was his wife still there?"

"Oh yeah, she's sitting in the back of a squad car as we speak. According to her, they were invited over for a glass of wine. I'd say she'll be all lawyered up as soon as she's charged. But the two of them, the Dwyer's, they're going to be locked away for quite some time. We're in the process of getting a warrant to search their home, should be coming through shortly."

"Don't forget to add that building down on West Seventh Street to the list."

"Already done, there's a team standing by to go through the place just as soon as the warrant comes through. Not that I expect them to be coming up with much. Those thugs have any brains they've already cleared out and are in the process of heading for parts unknown."

"You're giving them a lot of credit. Anything on Ozzie Frick?"

"Nothing you don't already know. He's dead. Shot twice, once in the chest and once in the head. The weapon that was on the desk in that room does not appear to be the murder weapon. We'll know for sure once we get the ballistics report."

"You going to be tied up with Burnsville all day?"

"No, I'm running on empty. I've been up for over twenty-four hours, and I need to catch some sleep."

"You're preaching to the choir on that one," I said and stifled a yawn.

"At this stage, I'm only going to be getting in the way here, I'm about to head back into the city. I'm still going to need you to come down and make a statement. Burnsville is going to need the same thing on your interaction with the Dwyer's."

God, I was never going to get a chance to sleep. “One more thing,” I said. “It just sort of popped into my head. We grabbed Molly Dwyer’s car. It’s a BMW. It was blocking Sophie’s car in the garage, so she drove it over here to the vet’s. The Dwyer’s were getting ready to drive off in the thing, once Dennis dealt with us.”

“Probably because they figured we’d be watching the airport. Where’s this veterinarian located?”

I looked at the building. The Burnsville Veterinary Clinic and the address numbers were attached to the front of the building in foot high steel letters. I read the clinic name and the address numbers off to Aaron. “Sorry, but I don’t know what street we’re on, it’s just a couple of minutes from where you’re at.”

“Someone here will know, probably be a squad over there in a few minutes,” Aaron said, then I heard what sounded like a long yawn.

“I’ll be inside in the waiting room, Sophie’s in with the doc, they’re doing surgery on the dogs. Maybe we can both get some sleep once they’re finished.”

“Can’t come soon enough for me,” he said.

I headed back into the waiting room. The woman with the little white dog was standing at the receptionist counter. Along with the soiled top, she was wearing a very wrinkled pair of cream-colored Capri pants, they had to have at least a forty-inch waist. “Is it going to be much longer? We’ve been waiting for over half an hour.”

"I'm sorry, we had an emergency show up, two of them actually," the receptionist said, then looked over in my direction. "Gunshots."

As she said the word, it dawned on me that I still had the gun I took from Dennis Dwyer. I pulled my phone out and called Aaron again.

"What?"

"Aaron, sorry to bother you again. I just remembered I've still got the gun I took from Dwyer."

"Obviously, we'll want that. Get it into something safe, so it's not contaminated any more than it already is. Someone will be over in a bit," Aaron said and hung up.

I walked over to the receptionist counter. "Would you happen to have some sort of large envelope or maybe a plastic bag?"

The woman with the white dog folded her arms, and shot a disgusted look in my direction. "Apparently, you're the reason we've been waiting," she said.

The receptionist handed me an 8x10 manila envelope and looked like she was about to say something. I set the envelope on the counter then pulled Dwyer's pistol from my belt. The eyes on both women grew wide as I slid the pistol into the envelope, barrel end first. With the silencer still attached, the handgrips extended out of the envelope. The woman with the white dog slowly took a few steps back then quickly waddled out the front door holding her dog tightly against her chest like a baby.

"Thanks for the envelope," I said. The receptionist slowly nodded but didn't say anything. I walked back out of the building and over to the BMW. The keys were still in the ignition and I took them out and opened the trunk. There were four pieces of luggage in there, two very large suitcases on the bottom and two smaller ones lying on top, all matching, all Louis Vuitton. I slid one of the smaller suitcases around and unzipped it. Even though I didn't really lift it, it seemed rather heavy. I peeked inside, neatly arranged plastic-wrapped bundles of cash filled the suitcase.

I closed the trunk then opened the rear door. Another Louis Vuitton bag matching the four in the trunk sat on the backseat next to a still wet bloodstain from Lilly. This was more of a duffle bag, large, with a brown leather handle and two brown leather straps running around the bag. It appeared more worn than the bags in the trunk. A zipper ran across the top of the bag, and I pulled it partway back before it snagged and wouldn't open any further. It still opened far enough that I could see inside. It was filled to the top with more plastic-wrapped bundles of cash.

Fifty

The receptionist said as she hung up the phone and flashed a nervous sort of smile. I had just sat back down in the waiting room and placed the envelope with Dwyer's pistol on the chair beside me. Would you care for a cup of coffee, sir?"

"You know, that would actually be great, it'll help me stay awake. Just black, please."

"Let me get that for you," she said, then hurried from behind the counter and disappeared around the corner.

I was thinking it was taking her an awfully long time to pour a cup of coffee when three police officers came through the door with pistols drawn.

"Please, keep your hands where we can see them," the first cop said. The other two fanned out behind him.

"Hey, I called you guys. Did you talk with Lieutenant Aaron LaZelle? He's a Saint Paul cop, heads up their homicide unit. He's over at the scene of that shooting on Frontier Lane. The pistol's in that envelope," I said and nodded at the manila envelope resting on the chair next to me. The handgrips on Dwyer's pistol were clearly visible.

"If you'd stand, please, sir, and turn around slowly."

I knew better than to argue. I stood, slowly turned around and placed my hands behind my back. A moment later, a pair of handcuffs were slapped on my wrists, and one of the officers began to frisk me.

"If you guys would just check with your people at the crime scene. They'll tell you I'm one of the good guys."

"What's your name, sir?" one of the cops standing behind me asked.

"Haskell. Dev Haskell. I'm a private investigator licensed to carry. My identification is in my wallet in my front pocket."

The cop who had been frisking me finished then stepped back and looked at the clothes I was wearing. He paused for a moment at the red Christmas socks then focused on the 'OFF' monogram on the shirt pocket. "Dev Haskell?" he said as his eyes darted from my face back to the monogrammed pocket.

The door opened, and two more cops stepped in. "Hey, Sarge," the guy who just frisked me said.

"Dev Haskell?" a voice said behind me. I turned and smiled at the guy with sergeant stripes. He was average height, with grey hair, a grey mustache, bright blue eyes, and a suntanned face.

"Yeah, that's me. I was just explaining to these guys that I'd called to let you know I had Dwyer's pistol, it's in that envelope," I said nodding at the manila envelope now in the hands of one of the cops. "I spoke with Lieutenant LaZelle from Saint Paul."

"Yeah, take the cuffs off, he's on our side. Sorry about that," the sergeant said as I felt the cuffs being released from my left wrist.

"Not a problem, I get it, you can't be too careful. That's Dwyer's pistol, and his wife's car is that BMW out front. I've got the keys to it," I said, as the cop behind me unlocked the handcuff from my right wrist. I reached into my pocket and handed the car keys to the sergeant. "Dwyer shot our dogs and we transported one of the dogs in the BMW. You'll see some blood on the backseat. It's from the dog. They're both in surgery right now."

"You shot Dwyer?"

"Yeah, in the knee. He was gonna kill us, but I was able to get the gun away from him then shot him so he wouldn't be going anywhere. I believe the paramedics are taking him to the hospital."

The sergeant nodded then said, "That Honda Accord out there yours?"

"Yeah, unfortunately."

"Let's have you come down to the station with us, and we can get your statement."

"Actually, my dog is in surgery right now, like I said, Dwyer shot him. I'd like to stay here if I could."

The sergeant nodded, then said, "Unfortunately, I'm going to have to take you to the station. We'll try and make this as fast as possible, get you back here so you can check on your dog. He's going to be under anesthesia after the operation, so we should be able to get you back here in time. We'll give you a ride," he said, making it sound like a generous offer.

I was going to argue then realized I had absolutely zero chance of changing his mind. So, I nodded and hoped they'd maybe forget about Sophie. He looked over at the cop who had cuffed me. "Take him back to the station, radio Benson, let him know you're on your way, and we'd like to get this accomplished just as fast as possible so we can get him back here. That work for you, Mr. Haskell?"

There was no point in arguing, and frankly, he was a lot nicer than he had to be. "Yeah, thanks, much appreciated."

"Good," he said then walked through the swinging door. A moment later, I heard him say, "Everything's fine, Marilyn. He was helping us. Where's the doc?"

"Let's bring you down to the station so we can get you back just as soon as possible," one of the cops said, and we headed out the door.

It was a ten-minute drive to the Burnsville police station. No one said anything on the way. At least I wasn't handcuffed. We pulled into a parking lot next to the one-story brick building. Like many suburban departments, the police station was in City Hall. A section of the building had a buff-colored stone front with a set of double doors. A peaked metal roof was over the doors with the word 'POLICE' in large white letters.

"This way, sir," one of the cops said, just in case I couldn't figure out where the entrance was.

Fifty-one

I didn't know if it was the pleasant surroundings, the fact that I was preoccupied with Morton's situation, that I was just too tired to care, or the fact that Detective Norris Manning wasn't there. Whatever the reason, I didn't feel the least bit stressed by the interview. The interview room was carpeted, with nice walls painted a sort of soothing beige color as opposed to the grey cinderblock walls in the city. The table I was seated at was a wood grain laminate, and the chair was comfortable and upholstered with a cushion I could lean back on. The room even smelled nice.

I guessed Detective Benson might be around forty-five. He wore glasses and had thinning salt and pepper hair that was combed back. He was fairly tall with a beer belly that hung over his belt. He wore a short-sleeved white shirt, a gold wedding ring, a wristwatch with a black leather watchband, and he had a blurry tattoo on his left forearm, an anchor with the letters U.S.N.

"So, you received the phone call after you drove to your home?" It was about the fifth time we'd been through this.

"Yeah, I was barely in the door when Sophie called. She sounded upset, really upset. I could tell she was crying, and I figured, Morton, my dog, must have done something like peed on her carpet or maybe chewed something up. She just told me to come to her house, and although she didn't actually say it, she made it sound like there was some sort of emergency, so I got out there as fast as I could."

"And you didn't think to inform Lieutenant LaZelle?"

"It never occurred to me," I said and drained the last of the coffee from the paper cup in front of me, my third. "When I got there and saw B.B.'s car in the driveway . . ."

"Molly Dwyer."

"Yeah, the girls call her BB. I guess it stands for 'Bouncy Butt.' I never heard her referred to as B.B. until Dwyer called her that this morning. Anyway, I saw her car parked in front of the garage so I figured something must have been really wrong. She answered the door with a glass of wine, which was strange because it was early in the morning, but I was so worried about Sophie, I didn't really pay attention. Next thing I know, Dennis Dwyer has a gun on both of us. He had shot our dogs before I got there."

"And he said he was going to kill you?"

"No, not specifically. Like I told you before." I wanted to say, *'Like I told you five times before,'* but I let it go. "Both dogs were lying out in the backyard, shot.

He told his wife to start the car, told us to get outside and to kneel down by the dogs. Not really rocket science at that point, he was going to kill us."

"So, you shot him?"

"Yeah, I got the gun away from him and neutralized him. I didn't want him getting away, but we had to get the dogs to the hospital. I shot him in his knee cap, and called Lieutenant LaZelle."

"So, why didn't you call 911?"

"It didn't really occur to me. Stress of the moment, I suppose. Figured LaZelle could get you guys out to Sophie's house, and we could still make it to the vet's. I didn't know how much time we had, didn't know how badly the dogs were hurt. Is there anything else? 'Cause no offense, but I'd really like to get back to the vet's and check on Sophie and my dog, Morton."

Benson seemed to think for a moment, and when he apparently couldn't come up with anything else said, "Let me get someone to take you back to the Vet Clinic. Keep me posted on how your dog's getting along, and thanks for your cooperation. Actually, Dwyer's been virtually untouchable for years. I'm sure we'll be the first in a long line of jurisdictions who want a crack at him."

"So, I'm free to go?"

"I'll have the tapes transcribed, and we'll need your signature, but under the circumstances, I'm not going to hold you here while that's accomplished. Come on, let's see if we can't nab a squad car."

I followed him out of the interview room.

“Oh, hey, Howie,” Benson said to a cop walking past. “You got a minute? I need you to run Mr. Haskell back to the veterinarian clinic.”

The cop eyed me for a half-second. “You the guy involved with Dennis Dwyer?”

I nodded.

“Nice work, man. Yeah, not a problem, I can have you back there in just a couple of minutes. Come on,” he said and headed for the door.

“Thanks again, Haskell,” Detective Benson called after me.

Fifty-two

The cop named Howie pulled to a stop in front of the veterinary clinic, hurried out of the squad car, and opened the rear door for me. There was a squad car parked out on the street, and a tow truck was in the process of pulling B.B.'s BMW up onto the truck bed to haul it away.

"Thanks for the lift, Officer," I said, climbing out.

"Nice to meet you, Haskell. We ever run into one another, I'll buy you a beer. Kneecapping Dennis Dwyer, that was nice work."

"I'm gonna hold you to that, the beer," I said, then hurried into the clinic.

This time the receptionist was all smiles as I came in the door. "Oh, Mr. Haskell, Morton is resting in recovery room two. If you go through the swinging door, I'll take you in to see him. Surgery was a success."

"Thank, God. What about Lilly?"

"She's doing just fine. We'll keep both of them here overnight then see about release tomorrow or maybe the day after. If you'll follow me, please," she said, then stepped away from the receptionist counter. I went through the swinging door, and she was waiting for me in the hall. We walked down the hall, past the two operating theaters, the doors were open on both rooms, and they were empty.

Gail, the doctor, was seated in an examination room with an elderly couple looking at the ears on a small furry brown dog. She caught a glimpse of me as I walked past and gave a quick nod.

"He's right in here. He should be coming around in the next thirty minutes or so," the receptionist said, in almost a whisper, as she quietly opened the door. Morton was asleep, lying on a white cushioned pad in the corner of the room. He had a white plastic cone around his neck that would prevent him from licking the wound. I could see the shaved area now just behind his front leg. It was very pink around the wound with a number of black stitches. "Have a seat, and I'll let Dr. Gilles know you're here," she said.

"Yeah, thanks," I said as she closed the door behind me. I settled into one of the chairs against the wall, watched Morton for a minute or two then drifted off to sleep.

"Mr. Haskell," a soft voice seemed to call to me from somewhere far away.

I slowly opened my eyes and came around. "What? Oh, hey Doc, sorry I must have dozed off for a moment."

"Actually, we let you sleep for about an hour. I understand you've had a busy night and day. Morton's just starting to come around," he said and looked in Morton's direction.

Morton sort of blinked awake for a moment then closed his eyes again.

"He's going to be rather lethargic for the next twenty-four hours. We'll keep him overnight and see how the wounds are doing."

"Wounds? He was shot twice?"

"No, thankfully. There was an exit wound as well, which turned out to be a good thing. No vital organs hit, but recovery is going to take a while, months actually. He'll be tender for the next few days and then slowly get up and want to walk. We'll set you up with a harness to use on walks. The normal collar might cause undue stress on the wound. Short distances, to begin with, let him set the pace. We'll get you all lined up before you take him home."

"How long before he wakes up?" I said.

He looked over at Morton for a moment. "He's going to be like this for most of the day. We'll keep a close eye on him if you'd like to go home and get some sleep."

"What about Sophie and Lilly?" I asked.

He smiled. "They're both sleeping peacefully. Actually, your Morton had a little better time with the exit wound. We had to go in and dig the round out of poor Lilly. She'll be okay, but her recovery time is going be a little longer. They're both pretty lucky. Usually, when a a dog is shot, it's some sort of hunting accident and we might see a few shotgun pellets. This is only the second time we've had something like this. We had a German Shepherd from the city's canine squad that had been shot about two or three years ago." He shook his head, remembering.

"And he's going to be like this for the remainder of the day?" I glanced over at Morton, his eyes were closed again, and he was breathing heavily.

"Pretty much. From time to time, he'll open his eyes for a moment but then go right back to sleep. All signs indicate he's going to be fine, but right now, he needs rest, and frankly, so do you."

"Okay, then doctor's orders, I'll go home and grab some sleep. Can I peek in on Sophie and Lilly on the way out?"

"You can, actually you can view them from the room next door. We've got it set up like that, so patients aren't disturbed during recovery. A lot of times, parents want to bring the kids in, and that's not always the best idea," he said and smiled.

I followed him down the hall to a small examination room next to the recovery room where they were. He opened some curtains covering a window, which immediately caused me to shiver as I thought back to some of the body identifications I'd done at the morgue. Lilly was lying on a white cushioned pad, just like the one Morton was on. She had a similar white plastic cone around her head. Her back was to me, and I couldn't see the area where the wound was. Sophie sat next to her on the floor, leaning against the wall, asleep. Even closed, her eyes looked puffy and red from all the crying she'd done. Being close to Lilly and knowing she was going to be okay was probably the perfect antidote for that.

Fifty-three

I woke a little after four that afternoon. I was lying face down in my bed, still dressed in the jeans, shirt, and red Christmas socks Aaron had taken from Ozzie Frick's closet. I slowly came to life, peeled off the clothes, and headed for a hot shower. After standing under hot water for twenty minutes, I began to feel halfway alive. I got dressed, put some coffee on and phoned Aaron.

He answered on the third ring, "You're a little late if you expect me to buy you breakfast."

"Sorry about that, I needed sleep, or I'd be no good to you. You get any sleep?"

He sort of snorted then said, "Yeah, I've only been in for about a half-hour. I can send someone over to give you a lift down, but I need that statement."

"Yeah, that's why I'm calling, I can be down there shortly. Thanks for the offer, but I'll drive myself."

"You sure?"

"Yeah, see you soon."

I filled a travel mug with coffee then drove down to the police station. I'd been waiting in the lobby for no more than a couple of minutes when Aaron himself came down and escorted me up to the interview room.

I'd been in interview room three more times than I cared to recall. Cinder block walls painted a depressing grey, a grey tile floor, and the metal-topped table with the occasional dent in it that suggested more than one head had probably been bounced off it. The difference between the room I was in now and the one in the Burnsville station this morning was like night and day. Burnsville was more like a nice hotel room, and this one, well the word interrogation rather than interview sprang to mind. Still, I wasn't feeling any pressure.

A metal cart on wheels with three shelves was pushed into a far corner. At one time, it held recording devices, but nowadays, all the interview rooms were monitored and automatically stored the recordings on computers. I'd been at this game long enough to remember cassette players doing the recording.

Today, Aaron had a laptop in front of him, along with two paper cups filled with steaming, disgusting coffee from a vending machine. Sitting next to him was blonde, beautiful, Norah Demming. A detective who had made it clear, on more than one occasion, that she wasn't the least bit interested in me. She had been in my house once, but only to meet Morton. I don't think she was there for more than ten minutes total, and only that long because we waited for two cups of coffee to be made. She didn't stay long enough to even finish her cup of coffee.

"Okay, so, let's get started," Aaron said, then typed in a series of commands on his laptop, waited a minute, then gave the date and time, listed himself, Detective Demming, and me. "And, Mr. Haskell, you are here at this time under your own free will to give a statement, is that correct?"

"Yes, it is."

"And do you wish to have legal representation at this time?"

"I do not."

"All right, let's begin with your voluntary involvement in the monitoring of the address at . . . " It went on from there for three more hours. At the end of it, I'm not sure who was more exhausted, Aaron or me. Detective Demming had left the room twice. She said she was going to use the bathroom, but I think she secretly just stepped out into the hallway and beat her head against the wall. Other than my shoe size Aaron covered everything else I could think of. We reviewed images of the tapes I'd recorded, and I made what comments I could, although at this point, most of the images simply ran together.

The one series of images I would have recalled was Swindle Lawless stepping into the porta pottie just before it exploded, but there was no video recording of that particular incident. That didn't seem to deter Aaron. He had me describe the incident I'd witnessed while hiding in the weeds. For the final hour of the interview, my stomach growling because I hadn't eaten served as the backup music for everything I said.

Aaron finally listed the three of us in the room, again. Then gave the time, brought the interview to a conclusion, and typed something into the computer in front of him that shut down the system.

Detective Demming breathed an audible sigh of relief then said, "If there's nothing else you're going to need, I should get back to my desk, things are piling up." She pushed her chair back, flashed a smile for just a nanosecond, nodded, and fled the scene.

"How come everyone in your department either wants to get away from me as fast as possible, or they're like Manning, and they want to lock me up for a hundred and fifty years?"

"I really don't know, you just seem to have that sort of effect on people, and don't limit it to just this department."

"So, where are we going to eat?"

"Eat?" He looked at his watch. "It's after eight. You're not tired after the last twenty-four hours?"

"More like thirty-six hours, but apparently, I'm the only one counting. In case you didn't hear my stomach growling during that interview, I'm starving, and you promised to buy dinner."

"Actually, I promised to buy you breakfast."

"Oh, yeah, my mistake. I forgot and skipped breakfast this morning, so I could get Dennis Dwyer arrested for you. Sorry."

"Okay, okay, Mickey's sound good?"
"It sounds like just what the doctor ordered."

Fifty-four

As we walked into Mickey's Diner, one of the waitresses gave Aaron a nod and said, "Hey, Lieutenant LaZelle, go ahead and grab that back booth. I'll bring you coffee in a minute."

Some guy waiting for a table said, "Oink, oink," just under his breath as we passed. If Aaron heard him, he didn't acknowledge it. I looked at the guy. He was maybe sixty, bleary-eyed and clearly drunk. He was with a woman a good twenty or thirty years younger. She was a home dye job blonde and had the hard-bitten look of a "working girl."

"Behave," she said to the guy, and sort of gave me the nod to keep moving. Actually, that seemed like pretty sound advice, and I just followed Aaron.

One of the nice things about Mickey's was that breakfast was served twenty-four/seven. I had scrambled eggs with bacon and toast along with a side order of breakfast steak. It was delicious.

We were seated in the back booth. I sat with my back to the rest of the diner, letting Aaron see anyone coming toward us. "So, all in all, it looks like shutting down Ozzie Frick worked out pretty well for you," I said.

"Yeah, we ended up getting Dennis Dwyer snagged, even if it was in a different jurisdiction. He'll be put away, at least for a while."

"Not to mention Ozzie Frick's place is shut down and a half dozen other sites that Dennis Dwyer operated."

"I have to say if that woman you mentioned hadn't brought it to our attention they'd probably still be operating."

"You mean Daisy, the neighbor lady yelling at folks with the bullhorn? Yeah, she was a piece of work. Funny thing was, it was Ozzie himself who brought her to my attention. He wanted me to investigate her. Thank God, it backfired on him."

"Big-time," Aaron said, then waved his arm to signal the waitress for the bill.

She came over a minute later with a coffee pot and the bill. "Hi Lieutenant, everything okay?"

"Great, as always," he said, then tossed a twenty and a ten on the table and stuffed the receipt in his pocket. "Keep the change, Madeline, thanks for taking care of us."

"More coffee?"

"No, tell you the truth, I'm looking forward to going home and crawling into bed."

"Don't I know the feeling," she said, then glanced at a large chrome clock hanging on the wall. "Three hours, eighteen minutes, and counting."

We slid out of the booth and headed for the front door. We passed the guy who'd made the "Oink, oink," comment earlier. He had an untouched plate of food sitting in front of him. His head was tilted back, resting against a window. His mouth was open, and he was snoring softly. It looked like the young woman had finished a plate of French toast and was in the process of going through his wallet, she placed a ten on the table, gave a quick look around then stuffed his wallet into her bag and followed us out the door.

I was parked maybe a half-block in the opposite direction, and Aaron turned to talk to me just as the woman hurried past. "Enjoy the rest of your evening, ma'am," he said and gave her a polite nod as she hurried down the street. "You heading home?" he said to me with a smile on his face that suggested he knew what she'd done.

"Yeah, first time in a long time, I get to spend the night in my bed. I gotta tell you, I'm really not going to miss that porta pottie."

"I can imagine, well, thanks again for your help, much appreciated."

"Let me know how the budget talks go," I said.

He smiled. "You can read about in the paper just like the rest of us. Catch you later, and thanks again."

I walked to my car and climbed in. Just on a whim, I phoned Sophie but got dumped into her voice mail. "Hi, Sophie, it's Dev. Just touching base. I checked in on you and Lilly before I left, but you were both asleep, and I didn't want to wake you. Hope she's doing okay, Morton's recovering. I'll be back at the vet's tomorrow morning. Call me if you need a place to stay. I'm guessing your house is going to be shut down for a couple more days."

I hung up, started to head home, and thought it maybe wouldn't hurt to stop for one at The Spot.

Fifty-five

I pulled around the corner at The Spot and parked just beyond the side door. As I climbed out of the car and started to walk in the door, a woman called from across the street, "Don't forget to lock your car." She looked familiar, but I couldn't place her.

"No one in their right mind would want to get in that thing," I said. She laughed, then waved, and I strolled into The Spot.

There were only about a half-dozen people in there. I stopped and said hi to a couple seated at the corner of the bar then headed for an empty stool halfway down in front of the beer taps.

"Hey, long time no see," Mike said from behind the bar. "Now I know why business picked up. You haven't been coming in."

"Thanks, Mike. Hey, just a Leinenkugel's for me."

"Already poured," he said, setting the glass down on a beer mat and sliding it across the bar to me. "Where've you been? You just missed Louie by about an hour."

"I was working a night gig for the better part of the last two weeks, looking forward to a little peace and quiet starting tonight."

"How's your better half?"

"I introduced you to Sophie?"

"Sophie? No, who's that? I meant your dog, Morton."

"Oh, Morton, let me tell you," I said and then did.

"You were involved with that explosion the other night over on the east side? And the arrest of that gangster out in Burnsville?" he said, fifteen minutes later, when I'd finally finished going over the details. As he spoke, he refilled my glass.

"Yeah, that bomb was meant for me, some crazy woman mistakenly triggered the thing."

"God. She okay?"

"Yeah, she's fine, amazingly unharmed," I said, not feeling the need to go over specifics of Swindle's shit storm explosion.

"And that gangster guy shot Morton? Stupid bastard better not think about showing his face in here."

"I don't think you have to worry. He'll be going away for a long time."

"Not long enough," he said, and headed down to the other end of the bar to take care of the couple I'd spoken to earlier.

I finished my beer then decided the sensible thing to do would be to head home. I gave Mike a wave, said good night, and headed out to my car. I climbed in, put my keys in the ignition, and was just about to start when a voice from the backseat said, "It's about time, Haskell.

I've been wasting a good portion of my life waiting for your worthless ass."

I half jumped, then glanced in the rearview mirror at Fat Freddy Zimmerman's reflection. Like I said to the woman on the way in, 'No one in their *right mind* would want to get in.'

"Hey, Freddy, long time no see, can I give you a lift somewhere."

"Don't be stupid, Haskell. What you can do is just drive around the corner and park in front of Mr. Gustafson's car."

"Actually, thanks, but I was kind of planning to just head home. Maybe I could grab a rain check and . . ." It felt an awful lot like a pistol barrel suddenly pressed firmly up against the back of my head, common sense suggested I didn't need to verify the fact. "You know, on the other hand, why not? I got nothing planned for the rest of the evening." My car finally started on the third try.

"God, this thing is a piece of shit. And what'd you have to pay to get a woman in the backseat?" he said and tossed a red bra up into the passenger seat.

I couldn't remember who it had belonged to or how long it had been back there. I pulled around the corner. Two houses down a black Mercedes, an AMG G-63, with dark tinted windows, was parked at the curb, Tubby's car.

"Pull in front of the Mercedes, and try not to hit it, idiot," Freddy said.

I felt like scraping along the side of the thing, but the thought of spending the next three months in the hospital in traction didn't really appeal to me. I parked in front of the Mercedes and turned off the car. After about ten seconds, the engine stopped sputtering.

"God, Haskell. For the life of me, I just don't understand how you make it from one day to the next. Okay, get out," Freddy said. He opened the rear door and sort of groaned as he oozed out of my backseat. I climbed out and closed the door behind me. Freddy shook his head and said, "You know, I actually feel sorry for the poor woman who was with you in the backseat. What'd it take, a disappointing thirty seconds or so? No doubt you finished before she realized you'd even started."

The passenger door on the Mercedes suddenly opened, and a very muscle-bound looking thug with dark curly hair walked around the front of the car to the street side, opened the rear door, and stared at us.

"Well, get going, Haskell, move your dumb ass," Freddy said, then sort of pushed me with the barrel of his pistol, which was about all of the incentive I needed.

I hurried over to the open door and bent down, about to climb in. The thug placed a massive forearm in front of me, then stuck the tip of his index finger under my chin and raised me back to the standing position. "You carrying, dumb shit?"

"No, sir."

"You sure? Because if I find out you're lying to me, you are going to find yourself in a world of pain."

"No, honest, check me out," I said, then stepped back and held my arms out in a crucifixion pose. He gave me a quick pat-down, rubbing his hands just firmly enough to leave me with the impression he was more than capable of doing some very serious damage.

"Okay, get your worthless ass in there." He sort of nodded toward the open car door.

"Thank you," I said, and climbed into the backseat.

Tubby Gustafson sat in the far corner. A little tray table mounted on the backside of the passenger seat was pulled down with a chilled stem glass sitting on it. A toothpick with three large olives rested in the glass.

Oh, hey, Tub . . . , err, Mr. Gustafson. What brings you down here tonight?"

Tubby reached for the glass and took a long, slow sip. "Ahhh," he said and smacked his lips a couple of times then looked over at me. "You know, Haskell, it's times like this I just shake my head and marvel at what a patient man I can be. Saint-like in my patience, that's what it is."

"Yes, sir."

"Which is why I have to wonder what, exactly, you did to my acquaintance, the late Mr. Ozzie Frick?"

"Your acquaintance? No offense, sir, but I was under the impression he was working for Dennis Dwyer, your, umm, competitor, sort of."

"And so that's why you had him killed?"

"Me, oh no, sir. I didn't have him killed. In fact, the police raided his place the other night, and actually, they thought they came up empty-handed until they found a pretty big stash hidden beneath the garage, and Ozzie was down there in a room lying in a pool of blood. Someone had shot him. But it wasn't the cops, and it certainly wasn't me, swear to God."

"Really, too bad. I was almost ready to congratulate you, Haskell. Here I was thinking there was an outside chance you acted as an upstanding citizen, doing your best to keep the streets safe in our saintly city."

I wasn't following. "Didn't you send Ozzie Frick to me because he wanted something done with the woman down the block. I sort of calmed her down, Daisy was or rather is her name."

"Really?"

"Yes, sir. She hasn't been harassing his customers lately, but I don't get why you wanted to help him out. I mean, he was working for Dennis Dwyer. My sources told me he was just a middle man in Dwyer's organization if even that. No offense and I'm not asking for particulars, but they were competition, right? And now they're out of business for all practical purposes and . . ." It suddenly dawned on me.

"Are you suggesting I'm involved in the illegal drug trade?"

"No, sir, and if it helps, I'm really sorry someone shot Ozzie."

"And you didn't do it?"

"No way, Mr. Gustafson."

"I suppose being able to spend your nights in a porta pottie was reward enough for you, wasn't it Haskell."

I had no idea how he knew, and I wasn't sure what was going to happen next. Tubby pressed a button, and suddenly, the window on the door next to me went down, and Tubby said, "Bruno, it would be bad for my image if anyone saw me with this idiot. Take him to his car, please, and get him out of my sight."

I wasn't sure what to expect. As the door opened, I turned and pleaded with Tubby. "Please, Mr. Gustafson, I didn't shoot Ozzie Frick."

Bruno grabbed me by the back of my shirt and effortlessly pulled me out of the backseat. "Go on, quit whining. Get your worthless ass into that piece of shit you're driving and get the hell out of here before Mr. Gustafson changes his mind." Bruno said. He held me up by my shirt collar, and I had to sort of dance along on tiptoes to keep up. We hurried over to my car, and I jumped in, mercifully it started on the second try. I pulled away from the curb, screeched around the corner on the next street, and sped home.

Once home, I double-checked the locks on the doors, wedged a dining room chair beneath the front and back doors, turned on all the lights on the first floor, then pushed my dresser in front of the bedroom door and crawled into bed. I was sound asleep within thirty seconds.

Fifty-Six

I remained in a deep sleep through the night and crawled out of bed just before six the following morning. I had coffee, and two chocolate cupcakes for breakfast, then got behind the wheel and drove out to the vet clinic to check on Morton, Lilly, and Sophie.

Morton was a thousand percent better, although somewhat subdued from what would be his normal morning behavior. He pulled away when I attempted to scratch him under the chin, and he whined a few times as he settled back onto his cushioned pad. Still, it seemed like quite an improvement. I'd been with Morton for about ten minutes when the doc came in. I was kneeling down, petting Morton.

Gail sat down on a desk chair, then rolled over to us.

"He's doing a lot better. We'd like to keep him for one more night, just to be sure. But, he should be able to go home tomorrow."

"He seemed a little skittish when I tried to scratch him under his chin."

"That's pretty normal, another forty-eight hours and he'll be more than happy to have you do it."

"How's Lilly doing?"

"I expect her to recover fully, but it may take her a little longer than Morton. Her surgery was a little more difficult, and she had a slight complication."

"Complication?"

"She's pregnant."

"What?"

"She's expecting," Gail said and smiled.

"Pregnant?"

"Just. Maybe a week along, two at the most."

I sort of frowned and did some quick math in my head. Morton had been at Sophie's for almost two weeks. "Are you sure?"

"Yes. With the stress of yesterday's events, the poor thing. I know Sophie was planning to breed her, but I didn't know she'd already done that, and well, I mentioned it to Sophie yesterday afternoon, and it seemed to come as a surprise."

"How'd she take the news?"

"Well, she didn't seem all that happy if that's your question."

"God. Did she say anything?"

"Not really, but I know her well enough to realize she wasn't pleased. It was sort of the icing on the cake for a very traumatic day. She didn't have a lot of time. It was the end of the day and she had to rush home and pack a suitcase. I guess the police are still keeping her house as a crime scene."

"Do you know where she stayed last night?"

"I think she got a hotel room. She was here earlier this morning, you must have just missed her. She had to go to the police station and give them a statement."

"Oh, yeah, I did that yesterday, while Morton's surgery was underway. Lilly is expecting?"

"Just," she said and smiled. "We gave her a quick exam after her surgery, given the circumstances she's healthy and should be able to carry full term, but right now the focus has to be on her complete recovery. A word of warning, it's been a very stressful twenty-four hours for both of them."

"Yeah, for all of us. Well, thanks for the heads up, it's much appreciated. And, thanks for all your help and dealing with us yesterday, you guys were nothing short of fantastic."

"We're all just happy everything worked out."

"Could I ask a favor?"

"What's that?" she said.

I pulled my wallet out and handed her my business card. "Would you send me all the bills related to Lilly's surgery and aftercare, please? I don't want Sophie to have to deal with it."

"Yes, I suppose we could do that but are you sure? They've been a regular here for the past three years."

"Thanks, but I'm very sure."

"Okay," she said, and read my business card. "Mmm-mmm, private investigator, that maybe explains a lot."

"Or just causes more confusion."

Fifty-seven

I stayed with Morton for a couple of hours, basically scratching him behind the ears while he remained on the cushioned pad. I checked in on Lilly for a few minutes, but she seemed asleep, and Sophie wasn't around, so I ended up leaving a message on her voice mail and drove back to town.

I parked in front of Daisy's house. I sat behind the wheel and looked three doors up the street to the cul-de-sac. All that was left of the porta pottie was a scorched floor and a few bits of blue plastic scattered around the lawn in front of Ozzie Frick's house. I didn't see any squad cars, and a police barrier had been set up across the driveway. Two black vehicles parked on Ozzie's front lawn had the look of unmarked police cars.

I got out of my car, climbed the steps to Daisy's porch, and rang the doorbell. I could hear what sounded like the tv coming through the open bay window in the living room. I rang the doorbell a couple more times but didn't get an answer. There was a light on back in the kitchen. I thought maybe with the tv blaring, she hadn't heard the doorbell ringing, so I wandered along the side of the house and into the backyard.

There was a small red brick patio up against the back of the house with a picnic table and a charcoal grill. Three wooden steps led up to the back door. The backyard was long and narrow, with a white picket fence running along either side. Well-tended flower gardens sat in front of the picket fence. A clothesline on the lefthand side of the yard ran parallel to the fence. What looked like two sets of white bed sheets and pillowcases, hung from the line. A single car garage took up the far corner of the backyard. A trellis of purple clematis stood next to the garage door. A mechanical sort of rumble seemed to be coming from inside the garage.

The back door was open, so I climbed up the steps and knocked on the screen door. I could see her dog, Axel sleeping on the hallway floor just beyond the kitchen. The tv was still blaring in the kitchen, and I was about to open the screen door when I heard a car door slam out in the alley and wondered if it might be Daisy. I hurried down the sidewalk to the back gate just in time to see a black Mercedes, an AMG G-63, with windows tinted so dark I couldn't see inside, driving down the alley. Tubby Gustafson. The mechanical rumble I'd heard sounded more like knocking or thumping coming from inside the garage.

I opened the garage door next to the flower trellis and stepped in. The overhead door was down and locked in place. A bare light bulb hung from the center beam providing the only illumination in the windowless structure. Daisy was standing in the middle of the garage with her hands on her hips, talking to some guy sitting in a lawn chair. His back was to me, but I recognized the thick, muscular neck and the dark curly hair right away. He held a tablet on his lap, and it looked like he was watching a cartoon, cars talking to one another, or something. With the four clothes dryers running and thumping in the garage, I couldn't hear what Daisy was saying. She suddenly stopped speaking, and her eyes grew wide as I stepped into the garage.

Tubby's thug, Bruno, from last night, turned around in his lawn chair, focused on me, and said, "Haskell? What the hell do you think you're doing?"

"Yeah? What in the world?" Daisy said.

"Oh, hi, Daisy. Umm, just wanted to check up on you, see if everything was okay. Sorry if I interrupted. Ahh, maybe it'd be a good idea if I came back another time," I said then turned to go out the door.

"Stop right there, dumb shit. Don't take another step. You are going to regret this, big time," Bruno said. He handed his tablet to Daisy, stood up from the lawn chair, sort of cranked his thick neck from side to side as he loosened muscles, and headed toward me. He was even larger than I remembered.

"Now, hold on, Bruno. Please, just hold on. I haven't done anything, so let's not get too crazy here."

"Oh, Bruno, for God's sake," Daisy shouted.

"This is going to be fun," Bruno said. He raised his hands and seemed to growl like some sort of grizzly bear about to attack. His eyes glared, and he flashed a wicked smile.

"Bruno, please," I said, backing up. "Now, just calm down and relax. There's no need to go psycho."

"You are about to experience some major pain, Haskell."

I retreated a couple more steps and suddenly backed up against the wall. "Bruno, please, don't," I said as he laughed and reached for me. I grasped for something, anything, behind me. The shovel gave off a hollow sort of thunk when I bounced it off Bruno's thick skull. His eyes crossed for a nanosecond just before they rolled up into his head and he crumpled to the floor.

"Oh, what the hell did you have to go and do that for?" Daisy shouted.

"Well, it looked like he was going to kill me, just for starters," I said and set the shovel down against the wall.

"Honest to God," she said, tossing Bruno's tablet on the lawn chair. The cartoon cars appeared to be chasing one another around a race track. "Come on, help me get him lying flat. At least, he doesn't seem to be bleeding. He starts bleeding on my garage floor, and you are going to clean it up, do you hear me?

"Just hold his head still until I get him straightened out," I said and grabbed Bruno by the ankles. I pulled his legs around, so he was more or less lying on the garage floor. A large red welt began to appear on the upper part of his forehead.

"You just keep an eye on him while I go get a glass of water. God, the two of you, absolute idiots."

"Maybe I should go get that glass of water," I said, thinking I did not want to be around when Bruno regained consciousness.

"You just keep an eye on him, I'll be right back," Daisy said, shaking her head. She hurried out of the garage and into the house.

Bruno was breathing, but he didn't move. I thought about hitting him again with the shovel just to be sure he remained unconscious then looked over at the four clothes dryers, each thumping along with a load spinning in them. They were white, looked brand new, and had the Kenmore logo on the door.

I walked over to them. They were front-loaded with a window in the door. I ran my hand across the top of one of the dryers. It didn't pick up any dust. Four clothes dryers in the garage, all on and thumping like someone had tossed a pair of shoes inside. I bent down and peered inside one of the machines. What looked like a couple of blue nylon bags were bouncing around inside. I checked the other dryers, they were all like that, two nylon bags spinning inside.

I opened one of the dryers. After a few seconds, it stopped spinning, and I pulled a nylon bag out. It was hot to the touch, and it took me a moment to undo and open the top of the bag. I peered inside the bag. It was stuffed with hundred dollar bills along with a couple of golf balls. The bills were counterfeits.

It was a standard way of 'aging' the bills. The golf balls bouncing around in the bag would give the newly printed counterfeit currency the look of used bills. I tied the bag shut, tossed it back in the dryer, and closed the door. The dryer started up immediately.

I noticed what appeared to be a pallet on the far side of the dryers with a paint-splattered drop cloth draped over it. I lifted the edge of the drop cloth with my toe. Stacks of freshly printed currency, maybe a foot high, were neatly arranged. The stuff looked so fresh, I wasn't sure the ink was even dry.

Bruno suddenly gave off a slight, raspy groan. I hurried over and thought about clubbing him again with the shovel. A large bump was just beginning to form where the red welt on his forehead had been just a few minutes before. It seemed to be taking on a purplish cast before disappearing beneath thick black curls.

I glanced toward the house, wondering where Daisy was. I could see her through the screen door, standing in the middle of her kitchen talking on the phone. The phone was mounted on the wall and appeared to have about a ten-foot cord on it. Daisy was pacing back and forth, laughing.

Bruno gave another groan and slowly moved his head from side to side. Fortunately he kept his eyes closed.

"Daisy, hey, Daisy," I called from the garage.

She glanced out the door then sort of waved me off and turned her back so she wouldn't have to look at me.

"Daisy, Bruno's waking up."

This time she didn't even bother to look at me. She just kept facing the other way with her back to me and waved her arm, signaling me to be quiet.

Bruno groaned again, then in almost a whisper, said, "Oh man, what the hell?" He blinked his eyes open, mumbled something else, and slowly rose up into the sitting position.

"Daisy, Daisy, we need you out here, like right now," I called, then reached for the shovel as Bruno turned and focused in on me. He moved his head slowly from left to right and blinked as if he was trying to remember why he was lying on the garage floor. He suddenly growled, "Now, you're really going to get it." He rose to his feet somewhat unsteadily, then assumed a boxer's pose and took a step toward me.

I grabbed the shovel and said, "Come on, tough guy, you want to try your luck again?"

Bruno took a step toward me, rotating his fists in circles and throwing the occasional practice punch. I raised the shovel ready to swing when, from out of nowhere, a glass of water appeared alongside me, and the contents were suddenly flung into Bruno's face.

Bruno coughed, sputtered, and backed up.

"You two idiots," Daisy shouted. "Just knock it off and stop with all the nonsense. Honest to Christ, Bruno, and Haskell, put that shovel down, now, or so help me."

Bruno looked at me, waiting for the opportunity to strike.

"And you, getting your head cracked open once already today isn't enough for you? Back up, Mister, take a chill pill and sit down in that lawn chair," Daisy said.

Bruno seemed to be having second thoughts.

"So help me, if you don't move your ass over to that chair right this instant."

Bruno gave me another look but didn't say anything, then walked over to the lawn chair, picked up the tablet, and grudgingly focused on his cartoon.

"My God, get out here, Haskell," she said and walked out of the garage. I hurried behind her then did a quick check over my shoulder to make sure Bruno was still watching his cartoon.

Fifty-eight

Daisy took a sip from her can of beer and said, "Mr. Gustafson and I have been . . . mmm-mmm, acquaintances off and on for a number of years."

'Acquaintances' with Tubby Gustafson, I physically shivered at the thought. We'd been sitting on her front porch for probably twenty minutes. She'd never offered me a beer. I suppose suggesting whatever conversation we had was going to be short and sweet. I kept glancing nervously at the corner of the house, expecting a half-crazed Bruno to come charging around the corner at any moment.

"Oh, for God's sake, will you just relax. That idiot knows better than to cross me."

"No offense, but I just want to be sure," I said then gazed down the street for a brief moment. A red flatbed truck drove past the far end of the block, and for a brief moment, I thought that guy probably doesn't have a care in the world. It was the same truck I'd seen a couple of nights back and figured there must be a construction project somewhere close by.

Daisy watched me then just shook her head.

"So, Daisy, no offense, if you don't mind me asking, but instead of yelling at people with a bullhorn and risking some sort of trouble from Ozzie Frick or one of those idiots pulling up in the cars, why didn't you just mention the problem to Tubby and let him take care of it."

"Oh, so, now you think I'm not capable of dealing with a local problem?"

"No, I didn't mean it like that. It's just that Tubby has, how can I say it? A pretty fair amount of local authority, especially with the likes of Ozzie Frick. I gotta believe a word from Tubby would have put everything to rest."

She seemed to think about that and smiled. "Sort of a double-edged sword, that nonsense up the street was under the auspices of a competitor."

"Yeah, Dennis Dwyer."

"Exactly. And the little bit of *service* I perform for Mr. Gustafson was in jeopardy while that operation was running. If Mr. Dwyer was aware of my relationship with Mr. Gustafson, there was no telling what sort of action he might have been willing to take."

I was about to ask her to define the words *service* and *relationship*, but then decided I'd rather not know.

"Well, I can't recommend the route," I said. "But the end result seems to have worked out. The cops shut the place down, along with a number of other operations, and it looks like your neighborhood will be back to normal. Pretty nice street now that there's not a car driving up and waiting in the cul-de-sac every other minute."

"Yeah, whatever normal is. At least you weren't injured. I watched you sneak into that outhouse every night, thought it was hilarious."

"You saw me going in there?"

She nodded. "Every night. Axel and I would sit out here right around midnight and watch you sneak in. I had to laugh, spending an entire night in there, night after night, you must have some strange hot buttons," she said and raised an eyebrow.

"But how did you even know?"

"How? Mr. Gustafson asked me to keep an eye on you, see that nothing happened, that you were safe."

"Tubby told you to do that?"

"Yes, of course, he's probably the major reason your little raid was successful. Not that the police will ever know and just a word of warning, I wouldn't tell anyone if I were you."

"But your little venture out there in the garage, participating in a counterfeit operation. No offense, but it's a federal crime. You could be looking at something like twenty years and a fine of somewhere close to a quarter of a million bucks."

She glanced at her watch and said, "Venture? What on earth are you talking about."

"Daisy? Four clothes dryers running in your garage with that thug Bruno standing guard, and you've got your laundry hanging out on the clothesline. Come on. I checked. It's not like you have a load of clothes spinning around in those dryers."

"I just love the smell of freshly washed clothes after they've been hanging out on the line."

"Yeah, great, but the dryers and Bruno out there watching his cartoon, it's not like he's doing laundry. Believe me, I'm not going to be telling anyone, but you might want to be careful."

"Maybe you should show me," she said.

"Oh, yeah, and have to deal with one watt Bruno again. No, thanks."

"Oh, his bark is worse than his bite. Besides, I'm sure he's gone by now."

"Why? Is his cartoon finished?"

"Let's go see," she said and stood up from her porch swing.

"No, thanks."

"I think you should follow me," she said, then walked over to the front door and held it open for me.

"Thanks, but no thanks. I should be taking off, anyway."

"Do I have to report your behavior to Mr. Gustafson? Tell him you took advantage of me? Threatened me with a gun after sneaking up and striking poor Bruno over the head with a shovel?"

"You wouldn't do that, would you?"

"Only if I have to, you should just follow me out back. Now."

I gave a long sigh then walked into her house. I was screwed.

"Just head into the kitchen and out the back door," she said.

I walked out the back door, Axel the dog looked like he was sniffing flowers in a far corner of the yard. He turned and looked as I opened the back door, then gave a growl and barked as he charged toward me. He stopped and sniffed me when I stepped onto the patio then sort of lifted his head, so I could pet him.

"He's always been a bad judge of character, come on, into the garage," Daisy said and shook her head.

"Ladies, first," I said then sort of held back.

"Oh, God, you can be such a pain. Come on, go," she said, then stepped past me and headed for the garage.

The inside was bright when we stepped in, although the bare light bulb hanging from the center beam had been turned off. The overhead door was open, exposing the asphalt alley just three or four feet beyond the garage door. The garage was empty, although the shovel I'd used to hit Bruno over the head was exactly where I'd left it. Bruno's lawn chair sat empty in the middle of the garage, and the tablet playing the cartoon was nowhere to be found. All four dryers were gone along with the pallet covered with the drop cloth.

"You were saying?" Daisy said.

"It's, it's all gone, it was, where the hell did everything go?" I said then hurried to the open door. I looked down the alley just in time to see the red flatbed truck with the dryers loaded on the back wait for a passing car, then make a righthand turn and disappear from sight.

"No idea what you were talking about, Haskell. Maybe it was you who got hit on the head with a shovel."

I reflexively rubbed my hand across the top of my head, then just looked at Daisy and shook my head.

Fifty-nine

I was at the veterinarian clinic by nine the following morning to pick up Morton. Sophie and Lilly were already gone.

"No, Sophie was here to pick up Lilly just as soon as we opened this morning. She's improving nicely," the receptionist said.

"Lilly?"

She gave a quick look then said, "They both seemed understandably anxious to leave this morning."

I was thinking it was awfully fast for the police to let Sophie back into her house. It would normally be listed as a crime scene for at least another day or two. "Did they go home?"

"I think so. Oh, and Dr. Evans said I should give you this," she said and handed me a number ten envelope.

I took a quick peek inside the envelope, the medical bills for both Morton and Lilly.

"Yeah, thank you. Now, if I could get Morton, I'm sure he's anxious to get home, too."

"I'll bring him out to you in just a minute, here is a list of post-op care items," she said and handed me three sheets of paper stapled together. "Pretty basic stuff, maintain his diet, make sure his water dish is full. Light exercise for the next fourteen days, short walks, nothing too fast, let him set the pace, and you'll need to keep the pet cone on for another twelve days. I think he's pretty used to it by now. I'll go get him," she said and stepped away from the counter. A minute later, she brought Morton out through the swinging door. His tail began wagging and beating like a bass drum against the receptionist counter.

"Hey, Morton, how are you boy? Did you miss me? I sure missed you," I said, then knelt down and gave him a long rub behind the ears. It was great to see him, and if it weren't for the pet cone, you'd never know he'd been injured just two days ago.

"Now, don't forget these post-op instructions," the receptionist said and handed me the instructions along with the number ten envelope with the bills. I thanked her, and we left, Morton hurried out the door just as fast as he could.

I put him in the backseat and noticed that he climbed in a little gingerly, but his tail was still wagging once he got settled. I drove over to Sophie's. There was still crime scene tape forming a large 'X' across her front door and a notice posted on the door. I didn't bother to get out and read the notice. The driveway was empty, so she was either staying with friends or was at some hotel that took dogs. I phoned her but ended up leaving a message.

On the way to the office, I stopped and purchased a new pillow for Morton to rest on. I'd placed the pillow in a corner near my desk, so I could keep an eye on him. It must have worked because he'd been asleep on it for the past hour. I was scanning the apartment across the street through my binoculars when Sophie called later that afternoon.

"Hi, Sophie, how's Lilly doing?" was how I answered when she called.

"Fine, it's going to be a while before she's completely recovered. I don't suppose you heard."

"Heard what, something from the police?"

"I only wish they'd get involved, no, Lilly was raped."

"What?"

"Oh yeah, Morton. He raped her, and now she's pregnant."

"Pregnant?" I said, hoping I sounded surprised.

"That's right. I have to tell you, Dev. Word of this gets out, and any opportunity to breed her is finished, done. As of now, she's tainted goods."

"You gotta be kidding."

"Oh, so, now you're suddenly the authority?" She sounded on the verge of yelling. The conversation was definitely not going my way.

"It's my understanding that in the eyes of the American Kennel Club, this in no way taints the quality of future litters."

"I'm well aware of the American Kennel Club's written policy. None the less, the clientele I deal with are the sort of individuals who value an untainted bloodline. It's what we all want, a purebred. It's one of the reasons Lilly has been so successful in competitions. She's a purebred."

Morton gave off a loud sigh and seemed to snuggle a little deeper into his new pillow. I took a deep breath and forged ahead.

"Where are you two now?"

"We're staying at my mother's for the next few days until the police are finished going over my home with a fine-tooth comb."

"Would you like to go out for dinner or maybe I could bring something over. Is your mom on any sort of dietary restrictions?"

"I'm not sure that would be the best thing to do just now."

"Look, Sophie. I'm sorry if you're upset about this, but under the circumstances, didn't it work out for the best. First of all, Lilly survived being shot, and second of all, you're safe. After that, nothing else really matters, does it?"

"Well, it certainly does in my book, Dev, and maybe that's just the difference between us. Since we started seeing one another, Lilly has been raped, impregnated, and shot. Lilly and I were almost murdered, and I've lost my best friend. I need things in my life to be correct, ordered, and none of that has been the case, as of late. You, on the other hand, seem to have no problem lowering what few standards you have just to get along."

"Well, Sophie, I'm sorry, but I disagree, I don't have a few standards. Actually, I don't have any," I said, and then laughed trying to move the conversation onto a more positive note.

"Oh, so, you think this has all been a big joke?"

"No, not at all. But I think you might just want to take a hard look at what you've just said and realize that the individual you choose to have a close, friendly relationship with might have led to the problems and incidents you just listed," I said, not referring to B.B. by name.

"Exactly," she said and hung up.

Well, that was that. I thought about calling her back then looked at the number ten envelope on my desk, the bill for the surgeries. I picked up my letter opener, ran it along the top of the envelope, and pulled out the bills. Emergency surgeries, Morton was $4500 bucks, and Lilly's ran another grand above that, no doubt due to the pregnancy exam. An even ten grand in medical bills. Another guy might have been mad, but me, a guy with no standards, I figured it was no big deal.

I went over to the file cabinet, unlocked it, and pulled the bottom drawer open. There was a bag in there, the Louis Vuitton from B.B.'s back seat. It was more of a duffle bag thing, large, with a brown leather handle and two brown leather straps running around the bag. The leather was worn with a zipper across the top of the bag.

I pulled the zipper about halfway back before it snagged and wouldn't open any further. There was still more than enough room to reach in. I grabbed one of the plastic-wrapped bundles, ten grand, cash. I'd run it over to the veterinarian clinic tomorrow.

My phone rang, I figured Sophie, given a moment to think, was calling back to apologize. "Hey, Sophie."

"Wrong again, Dev, it's Aaron. Sophie is actually talking to you?"

I let that last bit go. "Oh, Aaron, sorry. I was on the line with a client, and I guess we got disconnected."

"Yeah, sure," he said, sounding like he wasn't buying my explanation. "Hey, we got the results back on the ballistics test we ran on Dennis Dwyer's gun."

"And?"

"It's an exact match to the gun used to kill Ozzie Frick."

"So, you can nail him on a murder charge?"

"Not yet, but we can begin to build a case. One of the low life folks we picked up in the sweep will cop a plea, and then we'll have him. Dennis Dwyer will be going away for at least twenty-five years."

"Sounds like a happy ending," I said.

"It's heading in that direction. Just wanted to let you know. Gotta run, budget meeting, talk to you later," he said and hung up.

Morton sort of wiggled his shoulders and slowly opened his eyes. His tail began wagging the moment he realized he wasn't in the clinic. He slowly stood up and stretched cautiously.

"Hey, Morton, what do say we go for a walk? Expectant fathers need their exercise, too."

The End

Thank you for taking the time. I sincerely hope you enjoyed **The Office**. As an independently published author, I rely on you, the reader, to spread the word. So if you enjoyed the book, please tell your friends and family. Thanks again. Mike

Check out the following sample of **Star Struck**.

Sneak Peek

Star Struck

Second Edition

MIKE FARICY

Prologue

Delton Baggott looked around to make sure no one was eavesdropping on their conversation before he pushed the newspaper across the table and whispered to his brother. "I'm telling you, bro. They'll never catch on. You see this article, and he's right here in town, helped open that restaurant. Who in the hell is going to know, Clarence? We bide our time for the next few days. Find out where he'll be and make the grab. We just send a ransom note, and sit back 'til we collect the money."

Clarence nodded in agreement. He had to hand it to his little brother. Always coming up with a plan and, more often than not, they seemed to work . . . once in a while.

"I like it, man. We can make all the arrangements in here, put together a decent plan and no one will be the wiser."

"First things first," Delton said. "We need to come up with an out of the way place to hold him. I'm thinking that sleazy old motel out on Highway 5. The only folks that go to that place are probably renting by the hour. We could . . ."

Clarence shook his head. "Ain't gonna work."

"Why the hell not?"

"For exactly that reason. Everyone rents by the hour, suddenly we're there two, maybe three days, and wearing masks, telling the cleaning lady not to come in. Bad idea. We're liable to stick out like a sore thumb."

"You got a better idea?"

"Matter of fact, I do," said Clarence. "The lake place."

"The lake place? You kidding? No one's been there in at least two years. Hell, it's barely got electricity."

"Exactly. We head up there, make it livable, get rid of the mouse shit, turn the water back on, keep a low profile, no way anyone can track us. It'll be perfect."

The more Delton thought about it, the more sense it seemed to make. He was about to say something when one of the guards walked up behind them and said, "Okay, fellas, break time's over. Back to work, we need the entire mess hall mopped and then the hallway leading down to the cellblock."

They both stood, wiped their hands across the front of their orange jumpsuits, picked up the food trays, and carried them up to the counter. They slammed the trays against the inside of the garbage bin to dump the remnants before placing the trays on the conveyor. They made their way to the waiting mops and buckets in the far corner of the County Workhouse cafeteria. The room was large enough to feed two-hundred-and-fifty inmates at any particular time. At this moment, there were just three guards drinking coffee in a distant corner.

"Think about it," Delton said. "A few more days and we can take it easy for the rest of our lives." They smiled at one another, picked up the mops, and went to work.

One

I rang Heidi's doorbell Wednesday night, just after seven. She'd invited me over for dinner. She didn't mention it, but I happened to know the real reason she asked me over was she'd just broken up with her latest guy. I think they dated for six or eight weeks. I knew he was some high priced lawyer, but that was about all the information I had. Knowing Heidi, I was surprised she'd lasted that long. She liked things pretty black and white, and a high priced lawyer meant a lot of grey area, an awful lot.

I'd been through this before, close to a dozen times. The news of the break up would surface just after she got into her second glass of wine. On the first couple of breakups, there were lots of tears, but I hadn't seen any tearful reaction the last six or seven times. Now, it was just sort of a resigned sigh. She'd give me all the details over another three or four glasses of wine. Once again, I'd agree, whoever he was, he was really stupid, which actually was true. The night would conclude with an incredible hours long romp in her bed that would take me three days to recover from. I couldn't wait.

She answered the door wearing a tight white top about two sizes too small, no bra, and a skirt just a little wider than my belt. A diamond pendant dangled alluringly in her cleavage.

"Wow, what got into you? Right on time, for a change," she said, taking the bag with the three bottles of red wine. "Come on back, I thought we'd eat in the kitchen. I made ravioli."

We always ate in the kitchen, and she always made ravioli for these post-breakup dinners. I figured there must be something cathartic for her in the preparation process. By the way, the homemade ravioli was fantastic. The dining room would be off-limits for another two weeks as if she felt she somehow wasn't worthy. She set the wine bottles on the kitchen counter. I noticed she already had a glass going and made a mental note, number one.

"Oh, Dev, you are so sweet you always remember. A Sean Minor Pinot, my favorite. Oh my, 2014 vintage, aren't we special."

"Actually, there's three of them. I know you like it, and I feel like we haven't seen one another since forever. Guess you've been pretty busy. How are things going?"

"Well, with the economy going strong, I've been jammed at the office. Of course, the whole tariff situation is sort of hanging out there. There are predictions for everything from another recession to an even stronger economy. You know, I just keep my head down and continue working."

I knew for a fact, she'd forgotten more about the economy and business than I would ever know. She was smart, sexy, real sexy, and she could probably retire tomorrow if she wanted to.

"Here, I made some little hors d'oeuvres for us," she said, sliding a plate in front of me from across the kitchen counter. I had a pretty good guess what they'd be, goats cheese and prosciutto. It was part of her recovery process.

"Goats cheese and prosciutto," she said, taking one and tossing it in her mouth. "Do me a favor and open one of those pinots, okay?"

"You sure? We don't have to, and you can just hang onto them and save them for another night."

"The opener's in the drawer," she said, then drained her glass and slid it across the counter toward me. I opened the bottle, it was a twist off cap, then poured the wine through the aerator. It made a distinctive sound. Heidi took her glass, waited until I had poured mine, and then we clinked glasses.

"To happier times," she said and took a large swallow.

"Everything okay?"

"Yeah, not a bother. Come on, let's not rain on the parade."

I'd get the story halfway through the glass of wine.

It didn't take quite that long. Turned out, the guy was "a couple of years older" than Heidi. A partner in a high buck law firm downtown. He had a sports car, a lake place and, she found out, a wife and two kids. We were now finished with dinner, and Heidi was well into the second bottle of wine. Show time.

We were sitting on the living room couch. She was angled in the corner with her legs comfortably draped across my lap. The lights were turned down low, the drapes were pulled, and just in case things weren't morbid enough with Heidi asking a half-dozen times what was wrong with her, Leonard Cohen was playing on her sound system.

This is the way it always went, and after all the times I'd been through this, I was beginning to sort of like Leonard Cohen. Despite the morbid routine, he always seemed to eventually put Heidi in one of her sex-crazed moods, and tonight, I was going to be the beneficiary.

She drained her glass and reached for the bottle on the coffee table. She was slurring the occasional word and moving her head in a way that suggested it was a good thing she wasn't behind the wheel. She had passed the stage of using the aerator, and she filled her glass almost to the rim. She took a sip and dribbled red wine down her white top.

"Oh, shit," she said.

"Want me to get a paper towel or something."

"No, too late, damn it." She set her glass on the coffee table, sat up, pulled her top off and tossed it over her shoulder.

I didn't complain.

When her glass was about halfway empty she suddenly set it on the coffee table and said, "Okay, you ready?" Sounding like she was announcing the start of the second half to a football game. She swung her legs off my lap, waited for a few seconds to get her bearings, then shoved her hand around my belt buckle and led me into her bedroom.

The lights were off, but she already had a half dozen candles lit. A candle flickered on both bedside tables, and four more were evenly positioned across her dresser.

"Here, let me help," she said and proceeded to undress me. As I crawled onto her bed, she dropped her skirt on the floor, walked around the bed, and opened the top drawer on the bedside table.

"Ready?" she said, flashed an evil grin and then pulled out a large, battery operated appendage.

"Holy cow, Heidi, are you sure you can take that?"

She smiled, pulled out a black leather strap-on harness, and stepped into it. "Not to worry, sweetheart, it's not for me."

"Not for you? But, then . . ."

"Better take a deep breath," she said as she crawled on top of me.

TWO

The Green Door was a trendy, quasi-posh diner that served breakfast and lunch from six in the morning until half-past-two in the afternoon. It had a food and drinks menu, although, at just a little past ten in the morning, I was drinking coffee, black. Given the hour, the idea of a Bloody Mary or a beer sort of lost its appeal.

She saw me before I spotted her. Caroline Dillon, aka Caroline Travis, aka Caroline Moore, or, as I'd known her in high school, Sassy Aronson. If she was hot back in high school, she was scorching now, even after three marriages. She was dressed in tight-fitting Spandex leggings, black with a green maple leaf pattern, and nude-colored stiletto heels. Her small off-white top appeared to be strangling her surgically enhanced attributes. The top was low cut and barely covering. Her flat, tan stomach was enhanced by a multi-carat diamond that pierced her navel. She carried a double zip backpack that matched her Spandex leggings.

"Yoo-hoo-hoo, Dev," she called from across the restaurant and sort of jumped up and down. Immediately, every head in the place that wasn't already looking turned to stare. She headed toward me, strutting, one foot placed directly in front of the other, as if she were walking down a fashion show runway.

I read the lips on a fat guy two tables over. "Lucky bastard," he said and gave me the nod. I smiled back at him, then stood as Sassy approached. She leaned over and gave me a kiss on the cheek, followed up with a nibble on my ear lobe, stepped back, and scrunched her nose so I could admire her complete package.

"Mmm-mmm, you look great," she said, never one to tell the truth. She swung her backpack into the far side of the booth. I noticed it had a black leather patch stitched into the lower half of the pack with the name **marc jacobs**. I wondered if he was her most recent husband.

As she sat down, I smiled and winked at the fat guy.

He shook his head and shoveled in another forkful of syrup-soaked pancakes.

"Sassy, great to see you. How've you been?"

Not so much as blink. "Well, I suppose you heard. I'm divorced, again," she said, sliding into the booth across from me. She pulled a handful of paper napkins from the dispenser and a small spray bottle from the backpack. She misted some sort of disinfectant in front of her and began to clean the Formica tabletop.

"I might have heard something about the divorce. I don't really know any details," I said. I searched but couldn't find much more than an announcement on the internet.

"You'd think I'd learn, but these losers keep finding me. Fortunately, my attorney is very good. He's handled all my divorces, and when everything is all said and done, I've managed to come out okay."

'*Managed to come out okay?*' Clearly practice makes perfect. From what I knew, Sassy had never really held a job. She lived in an expensive top floor condo downtown when she wasn't spending the winter months in Florida or the Bahamas. She drove a dark blue Mercedes S 65 AMG coupe with a white convertible top. I couldn't afford the insurance, let alone the car, and on top of all that, she was head-turning, conversation-stopping, drop-dead, gorgeous.

"Hi, can I get you something, a coffee or tea. We've a nice chilled champagne?"

My waitress had suddenly been replaced by Teddy, the owner. A guy I sort of knew and who never, ever waited on tables.

"Mmm-mmm, I'd love a decaf tea . . ."

"Coming right up, I got just the one for you," Teddy said and grinned.

"Before you get that, can you tell me how it was decaffeinated?"

"How it's decaffeinated?"

"Yes, the tea, did they use ethyl acetate or methylene chloride? If they did, I wouldn't want to drink it."

"Oh, no, of course not. Well, I could check, I guess."

"Tell you what, maybe you better just make it a bottle of spring water, sparkling spring water. Pellegrino. I'll pour the bottle myself, please don't open the cap."

"Spring water," Teddy smiled and looked relieved.

"Pellegrino," she said.

"I'll be right back."

"Gee, sorry to hear about your latest divorce, Sassy," I said.

"Don't be. I took him to the cleaners. By the time I was finished, he was on his knees and willing to do just about anything to get a settlement. They always start out thinking they're going to win, and it always ends up the same. 'Course, Jerry Baker was presiding. He's been on the bench for all three of my divorces," she said and smiled.

"Jerry Baker? The same Jerry Baker you dated in high school?"

She smiled and shrugged.

I guessed the Honorable Judge Baker was in violation of a number of aspects of the law, and if Sassy's former husbands ever got wind of this, they'd have their attorneys filing appeals the very same day.

Teddy suddenly appeared with a glass of ice and a green Pellegrino bottle. "Your water, ma'am."

"Thank you," she said and flashed her brilliant smile.

"May I get you anything else?"

"No, thank you, I've my work out after this."

For a second, Teddy looked like he was going to offer to help with her workout. He smiled for a long moment and said, "Please, call me if I can be of any service. Anything at all," he said and started to walk away.

"Teddy," I called and raised my empty coffee mug. He sort of frowned, nodded, and kept moving. I turned back to Sassy, now rubbing a napkin around the rim of her glass before filling it with sparkling water. As beautiful as she looked, I was getting the sense there might be some issues that trumped her physical appearance.

She frowned and said, "Mmm-mmm, one too many ice cubes in the glass." She took a spoon and removed an ice cube, placing it in my water glass. She carefully poured the Pellegrino into the glass and took a sip.

"So, you said you were having a problem but didn't elaborate."

She nodded. "Yeah." She leaned forward and whispered, "I didn't want to say anything over the phone. I think someone might be listening in."

"Really? Any thoughts who?"

"That list is long. You could start with my three ex-husbands. After them, there are a number of individuals I've dated who were naturally upset when I didn't want to see them anymore. I've filed restraining orders on two different people. I suspect I'm being followed. I've had a feeling someone has entered my home . . ."

"Your penthouse?"

"Yes, while I've been gone. Now, all that said, at the end of the day it is still just a feeling. Nothing that I can prove, yet."

"Have you called the police."

"Yes, and they were absolutely no help. I thought, under the circumstances, it wouldn't be too much to ask that they station someone outside my door, but apparently they were simply too busy to aid a taxpayer in need."

I tried to envision the poor cop who had to take the call. They're shorthanded, underpaid, and not getting a lot of respect even on a good day. I couldn't come up with a positive image. "Okay, so what did you have in mind?"

Three

We had just stepped off the elevator on the twenty-third floor of Sassy's building. It looked like there were just two units on the floor, one on either side of the elevator. Both had a key-pad mounted on the door to unlock it. An antique credenza stood just opposite the elevator. It had a lamp on one end and a cut glass vase with flowers on the other, the flowers, mums, and daises, appeared to be fresh.

"As you can see, it wouldn't be that big of a deal if the police brought a chair and were comfortable while they guarded my door. I mean, I don't have a problem with them sitting down occasionally. It's not like I need them standing at attention all the time, but they weren't even interested."

I just nodded in response to her comment about it being no problem to station a cop at her door.

She input a five-digit code on the keypad, and the lock made a sort of grinding noise. She turned, gave me a sexy wink, and I followed her inside. The place looked contemporary, which usually isn't my thing, but I liked it. In the middle of the room was an open circular fireplace. A large copper dome hung over the fireplace, suspended by massive chains. The room had a white marble floor with a number of white throw rugs scattered around. The windows on the far wall were floor to ceiling, looked to be at least ten feet tall, and had a wonderful view of the Mississippi River valley.

A woman in a black skirt and top wearing a white lace apron suddenly appeared on the far side of the room. She was pushing a cart loaded with cleaning supplies.

"Oh, Carmen, I'm absolutely famished. Could you make me a piece of toast with marmalade, no butter? Thank you. Would you like something, Dev?"

"No, no, nothing for me."

Carmen rolled her cart back down the hall and disappeared through a doorway.

"Let me show you just one of the many things I'm dealing with," Sassy said, making it sound like there was a major hassle. I followed her around the fireplace, past the custom made white leather couches and down another hallway.

"Is there a bypass system to your front door lock?"

"A bypass system? You mean like a master code thingy or something?"

"Yeah."

"Not that I'm aware of."

"Who provides your security service?"

"A company named Elite Security, they were recommended. Are you familiar with them?"

“Only by name, I know they have a very good reputation.”

She opened an oak door with an antique brass doorknob. The oak trim above the door featured a pair of carved, classic comedy-tragedy theatre masks. “This is my entertainment center,” she said as we stepped into the room. There were three rows of four red, reclining theatre chairs, twelve in all. The floor sloped so that your view wouldn't be obscured by the person or the chair in front. A large painting hung on the wall opposite the chairs. She pushed a button on the wall, and the painting rose up into a slot in the ceiling, revealing possibly the largest flatscreen tv I’d ever seen.

“This looks really nice, Sassy. I’d probably end up in here all day long.”

“I can’t begin to tell you the difficulty I’ve had with this. I mean, is it too much to ask for proper sound and color?” She walked over to the tv and ran a finger along the edge, then looked at her fingertip, shook her head in a disgusted manner and sighed. “The dust, it just never ends.”

I followed her out of the room and down the hall to what I took to be the master bedroom. The walls were a pale-pink, giving the room a cold kind of feeling. The bed was large, at least kingsize, and had two steps to get up to it, almost giving it the look of an altar. A pink bedspread, just a shade darker than the walls, covered the bed. The bottom of the bedspread was edged with white lace. I counted six pillows and eight stuffed animals lined up across the head of the bed. A framed oil painting of three naked people embracing hung on the wall above the pillows and stuffed animals. A mirror, the size of the bed, was attached to the ceiling and edged in a large gold frame. Along one wall were eight louvered doors, each with a six-foot mirror, presumably, storage for incidentals, since the entrance to the walk-in closet was next to the double dresser.

"Nice room," I said.

"No, it's a lovely room," she replied, correcting me. She suddenly glanced at her watch. "Oh, my toast." She hurried out of the room. I figured I was supposed to follow, so I did.

Carmen, the woman who had prepared the toast, was nowhere to be seen. Who could blame her? The toast, one slice, was perfectly centered on a white china plate. A white linen napkin, starched and folded, rested on the grey granite counter next to the toast. The crusts had been cut off the toast, and neither the knife nor the jar of marmalade were in view. I was beginning to wonder where Carmen was hiding and if there was room for two.

Sassy took a bite of toast and closed her eyes for a long moment savoring the taste. She finished the piece over the course of the next five minutes and never said a word. I just stood there leaning against a granite counter with my arms crossed, watching. She picked up the linen napkin, wiped her fingertips, dabbed at her lips, and said, "So, what do you think?"

"It looked like a nice piece of toast."

She stared at me for a long moment, not sure what, if anything, she should say.

"Sassy, your place seems reasonably secure. You have an alarm system, monitored by a reputable company. You're up here on the twenty-third floor, so it's not like someone is going to get in through a window."

"There's always window washers?" she said.

"Only once a year, I don't think they'd be an issue. You have a secure entry. I'd be willing to bet that the police have a file on your unit. In fact, the cop you talked to probably looked it up while he was on the phone with you and decided that if they placed security just outside your building, you'd be better served."

"But I haven't seen anyone out there. Certainly, no police."

"Exactly. They want to be undercover, so they can arrest any potential intruder rather than have them see a uniformed officer and simply move on to the next target," I lied.

Amazingly, she nodded, suggesting I actually made sense.

Four

I was back in the office looking out the window through binoculars at a couple of shapely young moms pushing strollers down the street. They were talking and laughing nonstop. They wore tight shorts and loose tops. Both babies looked to be very young, and, for the moment, asleep, at least until it was time to eat.

Not a bad life, just eat, sleep, and your pretty mom changes you. You're too young to worry about the economy, the government, or how your favorite team is doing, and the most beautiful woman in your life lifts her top and presses you close a number of times on any given day.

My cellphone rang. I glanced at the name, a bunch of letters that didn't make any sense, but answered anyway. Amazing what one does to get business.

"Dev Haskell."

"Hey, bro, long time no talk," the voice said and chuckled.

"You're telling me. What's happening, man?" I had no idea who was on the other end.

"You're not going to believe it, but I need your help."

"What's the problem? DUI? Wife having an affair? Someone's husband after you?" I was trying to place the voice. He sounded familiar, maybe. But I couldn't put a name to it.

"Nah, this is cool. Anyway, need your help, I can even pay you a couple of bucks. An easy gig, and it'll be fun."

"What kind of help?"

"Tell you what, I just pulled up in front of this place. Have to run in and get fitted. You know where Painful Pleasures is?"

"Painful Pleasures? That body piercing place?"

"Yeah, just off of Seventh Street. I've got an appointment. Meet me down here, and I'll fill you in."

"Yeah, okay, it'll be good to see you again. It's been a while, we can catch up, and you can tell me what you've been up to in the last—"

"Gotta run, man, see you in a bit," he said and whoever it was hung up.

"You got some work?" Louie Laufen asked. He was my officemate, an attorney, currently sitting in his office chair with his eyes closed and feet up on his picnic table desk. He'd been asleep, snoring, until a few seconds ago, as he spoke, his eyes remained closed.

"Work? Yeah, maybe. If I can figure out who that was. The voice sounded familiar, but I can't place it. I just wish people would say who the hell they are when they call."

"Well, don't forget to mention my name if he needs any sort of representation."

"Not to worry, once I figure out who it was."

I picked up the binoculars, did a quick scan up and down the street, but the women with the strollers had apparently disappeared around the corner. After a few minutes of scanning the empty apartment windows in the building across the street, I set the binoculars in my desk drawer and quickly ran through my rolodex, hoping to see a name that would spark a memory. It didn't happen. I hopped in my car, a 2013 Jeep Wrangler that had been on its last legs since it rolled out of the factory in 2013. It started on the third try, and I headed off to Painful Pleasures.

Five

It was hard for me to envision a business devoted solely to piercings, although that's exactly what Painful Pleasures was. But then what did I know? I conjured up a vision from my high school days. Maybe a tiny dark room with someone's older sister heating a sewing needle in a candle flame before she stuck it in your ear lobe.

I walked into a contemporary lobby with a carpeted floor and a fancy cherrywood receptionist counter and a black granite countertop. A half dozen people were seated in the lobby reading magazines while they waited to have holes put in them.

The woman behind the counter smiled at me as I approached. She had a number of shiny silver bars piercing both her eyebrows, and her ears looked like there were zippers along the outer edge. A red jewel pierced either side of her nose, a silver ring with a green stone pierced her bottom lip, and when she smiled and said, "Hi, how may I help you?" I noticed there was a gold ball implanted in the middle of her tongue. I wondered if the TSA folks gave her a hassle when she tried to board a plane.

"I hope you can help. I'm supposed to meet a client here."

She nodded, smiled, and said, "And the name?"

"Mmm-mmm, that's part of the problem. See, he called me earlier this morning and told me he had an appointment here and that I should meet him. I just, unfortunately, sort of blanked on his name."

"Bono?"

"Bono? The U2 guy?" I said.

She nodded excitedly.

"No, 'fraid not."

She clicked some keys on the computer and said, "Mmm-mmm, if I gave you a first-name would that maybe ring a bell?"

"It might."

"Jeffrey?"

"No."

"Constance?"

"No, it's a guy."

"Luther?"

"No," I shook my head. "Unless it's, Wink. A guy named Luther Winkler, but I haven't seen—"

"Yes, that's the name he's using," she nodded. "He's waiting in room three. Oh, lucky you," she said, grinned and pointed toward the hall.

Lucky me? "Thanks," I said and headed down the hall. I hadn't seen Wink since, well, I hadn't seen him for a lot of years. We used to run in the same crowd in high school before we went our own way. Last I heard he was doing some sort of construction work, framing or something. He was a short guy, blonde, blue eyes, always sort of looking for an easier way to do whatever we were doing.

There were a half-dozen numbered doors along the hall. In-between each door was a framed black and white photo of piercings and jewelry, perfectly centered on the wall. The photos had been professionally taken. None of them were revealing, just ears, nose, lips, and navels. Actually, the images were rather nice, with elegant jewelry, but if a needle was involved, that automatically left me out of the picture.

If there was a gunshot, I'm probably your guy. But anything involving a needle, forget it. I can't deal with it. I had a couple of dates with a woman who was diabetic a few years back. We seemed to be hitting it off until one morning at breakfast she casually gave herself an injection after which she had to spend the next ten minutes bringing me back around when I fainted and fell off the kitchen stool.

It dawned on me that Wink was always pulling practical jokes on guys. If that was the reason he called, just to have a laugh as I passed out and hit the floor watching his piercing, he had another thing coming.

I took a deep breath and knocked on door number three.

To be continued...

Things are about to get very crazy. You better grab your copy of **Star Struck**, and catch up on the insanity Dev's got going…

Books by Mike Faricy

Crime Fiction Firsts

A boxset of the first four books in four crime fiction series:

Russian Roulette; Dev Haskell series
Welcome; Jack Dillon Dublin Tales series
Corridor Man; Corridor Man series
Reduced Ransom! Hot Shot series

The following titles comprise the Dev Haskell series:

Russian Roulette: Case 1
Mr. Swirlee: Case 2
Bite Me: Case 3
Bombshell: Case 4
Tutti Frutti: Case 5
Last Shot: Case 6
Ting-A-Ling: Case 7
Crickett: Case 8
Bulldog: Case 9
Double Trouble: Case 10
Yellow Ribbon: Case 11
Dog Gone: Case 12
Scam Man: Case 13
Foiled: Case 14
What Happens in Vegas… Case 15
Art Hound: Case 16
The Office: Case 17

Star Struck: Case 18
International Incident: Case 19
Guest From Hell: Case 20
Art Attack: Case 21
Mystery Man: Case 22
Bow-Wow Rescue: Case 23
Cold Case: Case 24
Cash Up Front: Case 25
Dream House: Case 26
Alley Katz: Case 27
The Big Gamble: Case 28
Bad to the Bone: Case 29
Silencio!: Case 30
Surprise, Surprise: Case 31
Hit & Run: Case 32
Suspect Santa: Case 33
P.I. Apprentice: Case 34
Rebel Without a Clue: Case 35

The following titles are Dev Haskell novellas:
Dollhouse
The Dance
Pixie
Fore!
Twinkle Toes
(*a Dev Haskell short story*)

The following are Dev Haskell Boxsets:

Dev Haskell Boxset 1-3
Dev Haskell Boxset 4-6
Dev Haskell Boxset 7-9
Dev Haskell Boxset 10-12
Dev Haskell Boxset 13-15
Dev Haskell Boxset 16-18
Dev Haskell Boxset 19-21
Dev Haskell Boxset 22-24
Dev Haskell Boxset 25-27
Dev Haskell Boxset 28-30
Dev Haskell Boxset 1-7
Dev Haskell Boxset 8-14
Dev Haskell Boxset 15-19
Dev Haskell Boxset 20-24
Dev Haskell Boxset 25-29

The following titles comprise the Jack Dillon Dublin Tales series:

Welcome
Jack Dillon Dublin Tale 1
Sweet Dreams
Jack Dillon Dublin Tale 2
Mirror Mirror
Jack Dillon Dublin Tale 3
Silver Bullet
Jack Dillon Dublin Tale 4
Fair City Blues
Jack Dillon Dublin Tale 5

Spade Work
Jack Dillon Dublin Tale 6
Madeline Missing
Jack Dillon Dublin Tale 7
Mistaken Identity
Jack Dillon Dublin Tale 8
Picture Perfect
Jack Dillon Dublin Tale 9
Dublin Moon
Jack Dillon Dublin Tale 10
Mystery Woman
Jack Dillon Dublin Tale 11
Second Chance
Jack Dillon Dublin Tale 12
Payback Brother
Jack Dillon Dublin Tale 13
The Heist
Jack Dillon Dublin Tale 14
Jewels To Kill For
Jack Dillon Dublin Tale 15
Retirement Scheme
Jack Dillon Dublin Tale 16
The Collector
Jack Dillon Dublin Tale 17

Jack Dillon Dublin Tales Boxsets:

Jack Dillon Dublin Tales 1-3
Jack Dillon Dublin Tales 4-6
Jack Dillon Dublin Tales 1-5

Jack Dillon Dublin Tales 1-7
Jack Dillon Dublin Tales 6-10

The following titles comprise the Hotshot series;

Reduced Ransom! Second Edition
Finders Keepers! Second Edition
Bankers Hours Second Edition
Chow Down Second Edition
Moonlight Dance Academy Second Edition
Irish Dukes (Fight Card Series)
written under the pseudonym Jack Tunney

The following titles comprise the Corridor Man series:

Corridor Man
Corridor Man 2: Opportunity knocks
Corridor Man 3: The Dungeon
Corridor Man 4: Dead End
Corridor Man 5: Finger
Corridor Man 6: Exit Strategy
Corridor Man 7: Trunk Music
Corridor Man 8: Birthday Boy
Corridor Man 9: Boss Man
Corridor Man 10: Bye Bye Bobby

Corridor Man novellas:

Corridor Man: Valentine
Corridor Man: Auditor
Corridor Man: Howling

Corridor Man: Spa Day

The following are Corridor Man Boxsets:

Corridor Man Boxset 1-3
Corridor Man Boxset 1-5
Corridor Man Boxset 6-9

All books are available on Amazon.com

Thank you!

Contact the author:

- Email: mikefaricyauthor@gmail.com
- Twitter: @Mikefaricybooks
- Facebook: Mike Faricy Author
- Website: http://www.mikefaricybooks.com

Published by

MJF Publishing

www.ingramcontent.com/pod-product-compliance
Lightning Source LLC
Chambersburg PA
CBHW071411200726
48294CB00002B/359

9781962080231